ANOTHER CHANCE

WENDY SMITH

Edited by
CREATING INK
Cover Design by
BOOKISH GRAPHICS

Content Warning: Fat shaming and death from cancer

1

CASSIE

They're fighting again.

I might be the biggest nerd in the school—we're at the end-of-year school ball which I'm only here because I have to be as dux—but the whispers don't bypass me.

The gossip chain's been rumbling for a while about Patrick Cross—the school rugby captain—and his girlfriend, Vicki, being on the verge of breaking up.

And tonight it's obvious.

Patrick used to be my best friend. All the way through, up until we hit high school, we were inseparable. But at that point, he became the cool kid and I was left behind.

Tonight's argument between him and his girlfriend is because of me.

About ten minutes ago, in the car park outside the school hall, I ran into Patrick and Vicki. She glared at me the way she always does, and he, for the first time since we were about thirteen, decided I was worthy of his attention.

That's probably a little unfair—he's not a bad person. But he's neglected our friendship for almost five years, and for him to stop and speak to me for more than a moment or two was weird.

What made it weirder, and Vicki angrier, was when he told me to save a dance for him.

She had a dig at my weight—Vicki loves the fat jokes—and he snapped at her to be quiet.

And now this.

From the other side of the hall, I can't help but watch. She's gesticulating wildly, her arms waving around as if they're telling a story all of their own.

He's standing there with his arms folded across his broad chest, his lips in a straight line when he's not spitting words at her.

Even if things are bad between them, I never thought they'd argue in public. Again.

I didn't see it a few days ago, but I heard whispers.

Maybe it's because we're about to finish school for good and head off to university. Our different levels of maturity are obvious now.

There are still those who subscribe to the mean-girl mentality—Vicki is one of them.

The evening's still got a way to go, but I'm done with it tonight. I'm not one for dressing up and going out to start with—I doubt the fancy cream gown I'm wearing will ever be worn again. It's been nice to pamper myself a bit, but I'm also dateless, so I feel a bit like a fish out of water with everyone else paired up.

Patrick's gaze hits mine, and my heart thuds.

I look away—despite the years, his neglect of our friendship still hurts.

It's time to go.

I've only taken a few steps when I hear him behind me.

"Cassie. Wait."

I turn. Patrick jogs around the edge of the dance floor to get to me.

"Dance with me?"

I shift my gaze over his shoulder to his very unimpressed-looking girlfriend. "Do you really think this is a good idea?"

"It might be the last chance we get before school finishes."

"I …" I don't have any real excuses not to. We were best friends once—inseparable. And he's right. This might be the one and only chance I have to dance with the boy I've been in love with since I was five years old. "Sure."

His face lights up, and he reaches for my hand.

It's a slower song, not the kind that you cuddle up for, but slow enough that Patrick wraps his arms around my waist as I slip mine around his neck.

"This is nice."

"Is this what you were arguing about?"

His eyebrows rise. He's not used to me being blunt. I spent so many years tiptoeing around him and everyone else in the hopes I'd be left alone.

But I've got no energy left for that.

"Things aren't good."

"I'm sorry to hear that." And I am. Because I still care despite him not seeming to.

"It is what it is. I won't be here next year anyway, and if we can't get on now, I doubt we'd survive long-distance."

I tilt my head. "Really?"

"I've been thinking a lot about the future and how things have to change."

My heart leaps. Even if I'm not a part of that future, I'm proud of him.

His gaze hits mine. "I miss you."

I snort. "I didn't think you'd noticed."

"Of course I did. I'm just a little slow to wake up to what I've been doing—or what Vicki and her friends have been doing. You never complained to me about their bullying."

No, I didn't.

I could have—I knew that, but I figured there was very little point. My friendship with Patrick seemed to have run its course, and there was a part of me that was scared that he would agree and join in.

"It's fine."

"No, it's not." His blue eyes are piercing. "I'm done with this immature bullshit. Someone in Vicki's friend group told me she's always picked on you, but I'd told her a long time ago that you were off limits."

Tears prick my eyes. He didn't protect me, but he thought he had?

"I'm not sure I want to get into this now."

His jaw tightens, and he nods. "That's fair enough. But this isn't over. I can't begin to tell you how angry I am right now. I—"

"If I'd told you, would it have made a difference?"

His brow furrows. "Of course it would."

I swallow hard. Where did everything go wrong? For the past five years, I thought he was embarrassed to be my friend, and now he comes out with this, and he's dancing with me.

The song finishes, and I force a smile. "Thanks for the dance. I think I'm going to go home."

He nods and drops his hands. "I'm sorry, Cassie. For everything."

"School's over soon. And then I'll never have to deal with her again." I sigh. "Goodnight, Patrick."

"See you soon?"

I shrug.

He frowns, but I turn and walk away.

There's no point dwelling in the past.

I can't let it influence my future.

I'm done.

———

It's still early when I pull into my driveway.

I open the front door and step in.

"Cassie," Mum calls from the living room. "Come and tell us all about it."

I close my eyes for a moment.

Shit.

I'd hoped to sneak in without a fuss.

I turn and step into the room. Dad's glued to the television and barely looks at me—he won't interrogate me about tonight—but Mum sits, knitting needles poised with an expectant look on her face.

"How was it?" she asks.

I shrug. "Fine."

She tilts her head and pats the couch beside her. I sigh and flop down onto it.

"Only fine?"

"I don't know what else to say. Everyone was all dressed up, and the principal's speech wasn't popular because he stopped the dancing to give it."

She laughs. "I can imagine. Who wants to listen to that in the middle of a party."

"I danced with Patrick."

Her eyes light up. "You did? I hope that means things are good between you."

It was Mum's shoulder I cried on when Patrick pulled away. We'd been joined at the hip for so long, I had no girl friends to depend on.

"I'm not sure, but I don't think he'll be with Vicki for much longer."

"Really?"

I nod. "He didn't sound too happy. But I don't know. I'll believe it when I see it."

Mum squeezes my arm. "It seems like he's coming to his senses. That's way overdue."

"Maybe." I shrug. "All I know is that in a month's time when school is over, I'll never have to deal with the drama again."

Why do I feel like those are famous last words?

2

PATRICK

My girlfriend is a duplicitous bully.

She used to be all sunshine and rainbows with me, but I never liked the side of her that gossiped.

Over time, that became all she ever did.

I've not been happy for a while and have been thinking of breaking things off, but the night of the school dance sealed the deal.

I wondered how much else she'd done in the past.

Three years ago, Dave Pratt—who was a friend—played a prank on Cassie that horrified me. I punched him in the face for it, and things haven't been the same between us since.

But now I'm rethinking what happened.

That night, Vicki told me she wasn't feeling well, so I stayed home and I thought she had too. It turned out that she was there—though she told me she had nothing to do with it and was just a witness.

We still fought because she did nothing to help Cassie.

After our argument the night of the dance, with increasing doubts in my mind, I approach Dave.

He visibly draws in a deep breath, wariness in his eyes as I draw near.

I don't blame him—we've rarely talked.

But I have to know.

"You summoned me?" His attitude has always pissed me off. I sent him a text earlier asking him to meet up in the park, and he was reluctant at first. But I pressed the issue and told him I needed his help.

He takes a seat beside me on a park bench.

"I need to know how involved Vicki was in your prank on Cassie."

He rolls his eyes. "Oh, now the golden boy is interested in what happened."

"Please, Dave. It's important.

His expression straightens. "It was her idea."

My jaw clenches. I'd half expected to hear it, but him confirming it is a whole other story. "What happened?"

He shrugs. "You hadn't been together long and she was jealous that you two used to be friends."

Used to be friends? That makes my heart ache. I've never thought about Cassie as a former friend—we just wanted different things.

Dave holds up his palms. "She told me that you hated Cassie. That you'd had some big falling out and you were looking for payback."

"You didn't think to ask *me* about it?"

"You and Vicki were tight. Vicki said you didn't want to be a part of it because Cassie's parents knew yours." He snorts. "Besides, her bestie, Kelly, gave me a hand job. That sealed the deal."

I shake my head. "I had no idea."

"Yeah, I got that when you came after me. You never asked, so I never bothered telling you."

I run my fingers through my hair.

He nudges my arm. "You know that's not all, right? Vicki barely left Cassie alone at times."

"No, I didn't know. She hid it well."

"Nothing as obvious as that prank. But plenty of nasty words. She might be hot, but she's a bully."

I fist my hand in frustration and flex. "I knew that she and her friends gossiped—it drove me mad, but I thought that was it."

"Well, now you know."

I nod. "Thanks, Dave. I appreciate it."

He sighs. "For what it's worth, Cassie didn't deserve it—I know that. I think I knew it even then, but those girls use what they've got for evil."

"It sounds like it."

"If you weren't so busy playing all your sport and studying, you might have noticed more."

I scrub my face with my hands. "I let her down so badly. I'm really hoping I can make up for it now."

"Just keep Vicki away from her until the end of summer. Then you and Cassie can sail off into the sunset together."

I laugh. "I don't want to get ahead of myself."

"She deserves better—whatever that is. And you guys are lucky you're getting out of here."

I raise my eyebrows. "You're staying here?"

"Dad wants me to work on the orchard. You know me, I'm not really academic. But I'll stay and work a year and see how things go." He drops his gaze. "It might help if I knew what to do with my life. You've always been so together."

"I'm not sure about that." It's true that I've wanted to be a doctor for a long time—it was something Cassie and I had in common. But along the way, I wanted to do a ton of other things as well. "I told Mum once I wanted to be an astronaut."

He chuckles. "You probably would have killed it. I suck at everything."

"Nah." I bump his shoulder. "Thank you for telling me the truth."

Dave frowns. "I should have told you a long time ago. What are you going to do?"

I lean back and stretch. "Break up with Vicki for good."

———

VICKI'S EXPECTING ME.

Things have been so strained that we have barely been speaking. So when I sent her a text to say I was coming over, she replied faster than I'd expected.

I've got a sinking feeling she thinks I'm going to make up with her.

Her mother smiles warmly when she opens the front door. "Hi, Patrick. Come in. She's out the back by the pool."

Of course she is.

I pinch the bridge of my nose and stroll through the house until I reach the ranch slider leading to the deck.

It's like a scene from a magazine.

Vicki's stretched out on a lounger by the pool in a white bikini, one arm up behind her.

She lies there, her eyes closed as if she doesn't know I'm here.

I'd bet anything she does.

"Vicki." I step out onto the deck.

She turns her head, a wide smile on her face.

I take another step and come to a halt.

Vicki pushes herself up and then runs toward me.

"Hey." She's breathless like she's excited to see me, but she must be worried. Every time we're together we argue.

"We need to talk."

She swallows hard.

"Why don't we take a seat?" I nod toward the nearby table and chairs.

"What's this about?" She flutters her eyelashes at me when we're seated opposite each other.

"I spoke with Dave. Confirmed a few things I suspected. I can't believe you got up to all these nasty things behind my back."

"Oh, please," she snaps. "You didn't see it because you didn't want to."

"That's not true. I thought you actually gave a shit about my feelings, and I told you specifically that Cassie was off limits. It turns out you did the exact opposite."

Vicki glares at me.

"I trusted you. And I really thought you were better than that. I guess I never knew you at all."

She swallows hard. Anger flashes across her face before she flutters her eyelashes at me again. "It really wasn't that bad. Did Cassie complain?"

The pit of my stomach coils. "No, she didn't. And I'm

telling you now that I'll be watching. You don't go near her. Ever."

She schools her expression. "So we're okay?"

"No. God no. We are done. So done."

Panic flares in her eyes. "We can't be. Not because of her."

"It's not because of her. It's because of *you*." I grit my teeth together. "She never did a thing to you. We are over, Vicki. And you only have yourself to blame."

She reaches for my forearm, but I pull away.

I roll my eyes as she lets out a loud, dramatic sob.

"No, I'm not falling for this. You made your bed. You can lie in it."

"You're really throwing us away?" She sniffs.

"You did that."

Before she can say anything else, I walk out.

"Patrick."

She runs after me, grabbing at my arm again.

"Go away, Vicki. I can't even look at you."

"We had something special, didn't we?"

I close my eyes and try to push the anger down. "We used to. Or at least, I thought we did. Now I'm not sure I believe any of it."

She lets me go, and I stroll away.

This time, for good.

$$3$$

CASSIE

A month later, it's the last day of school.

I've seen Patrick around and heard more rumours about him splitting with Vicki. But with the year winding up and final exams over, school's a lot more casual and I haven't noticed much of either of them.

But today, even though it's out of season, the other local high school have sent over their rugby team for a fun match.

It feels like there are hundreds of people here to watch—I think the whole school turned out. And I wouldn't normally bother but, even though he lives right across the road from me, this might be my best chance to see Patrick for the last time.

I don't know where he's going to university, but I know he'll be going. A part of me hopes it's Auckland like me, but then again, does that mean I'd still be pulled by these unrequited feelings I have for him?

It'd probably be for the best if we went our separate ways —for my sake.

That doesn't stop my heart from soaring as he leads his team out onto the field. I'm up in the bleachers at one side of the field. It's about as far as you can get from the play but still see what's happening.

It's not school pride—it's the deep love that I've always had for him that breaks to the surface.

A cheer goes up, and to the left of me someone wolf whistles.

I turn my head in the direction of the sound and meet Vicki's angry gaze.

Great. That's all I need.

Thankfully, there's half a row of people between us and she can't get at me until the end of the game—no one's giving up their seat at half-time.

It's late December, so the sun is warm and the ground is hard. It's supposed to be a fun game, but when the players hit the ground, it's hard not to recoil when the sound echoes over the field.

Music booms from the school sound system, making it a party atmosphere.

For the first time in a long time while on the school grounds, I relax.

And when our team wins, I smile wide because no matter how much I dislike high school, I'm proud.

The crowd thins as the teams switch shirts.

I can't take my eyes from Patrick as he lifts his over his head. Even from a distance, his chest is amazing, the hills and valleys of his abs prominent as my breath quickens. The guy is perfect—over six foot, dark haired and blue eyed. It's impossible not to be impressed by him.

A loud laugh comes from my left.

Ugh.

I'd almost forgotten about them.

Vicki snorts. "There's no way you think he's interested in you."

I close my eyes and take a deep breath.

When I open them again, Patrick's walking toward the bleachers. He's still shirtless, carrying the opposition's number 7 shirt in his hand.

I can't watch this.

I can't see him make up with Vicki right in front of me.

"He's coming for you, Vicki," one of her toxic friends crow.

Oh, great.

I pick up my bag, sling it over my shoulder, and step down two rows before Patrick calls out.

"Cassie. Wait."

I reach the base of the bleachers and pause.

Patrick jogs the last few metres and comes to a stop in front of me. "Hey."

He beams a smile that I'm sure blinds everyone in a 20-metre radius.

My heart races. "Hi?"

"I … uhh … I wondered if you wanted this?"

My eyebrows rise when he holds up the shirt he's just taken from the opposing player. I get the sentiment, and it's sweet, but doubt rises in me and I can't help myself.

"You thought I'd like a stinky shirt?"

He laughs. "When you put it like that … Maybe I just wanted an excuse to talk to you."

Someone snorts behind me, but I ignore it.

"You never needed an excuse."

His dimples pop when his smile grows. I bark out a laugh as he grabs my hand and pulls me down onto a bench. I'm well aware we're being watched, but he doesn't seem to care.

"I should have asked you the other night. Are you still going to Auckland Uni?"

I nod.

"We're moving to Auckland at the end of January. Mum and Dad bought a house up there. I'm really glad you're going there too."

He's so full of enthusiasm, and it's catching.

"I can't wait to get out of here."

His eyes search mine. "Me too. It's a fresh start."

I force a smile.

"That's how I feel."

"I want to spend my summer with you. I mean, if you want to hang out. It's been too long."

My throat tightens and I'm not sure how I'm still breathing, the way my whole body's reacting to him.

"I … I'd love to."

Swallowing down my fears won't be easy, but I have to have some faith in him. He hasn't so much as glanced in Vicki's direction, and his entire attention is focused on me.

He beams. "Good. Now, I've got to go and get dressed and get out of here. Do you have much to grab? I can help if you want?"

I shake my head. "Just some final bits and pieces from my locker. I'll be fine."

Leaning forward, he pops a kiss on my cheek. My skin burns from the contact, and he sits back and gives my knee a squeeze. "Okay. Catch up with you later."

For a moment, I'm dazed as he walks away.

Did I slip into a parallel universe?

I'm at a loss to understand this change in behaviour, and I'm not really sure I trust him yet.

Did that really just happen?

I grab my bag and start the walk back to my locker only to run straight into Vicki.

"Do you really think he's interested in you?" she asks.

"Just get straight to the point, why don't you?" I roll my eyes and tumble the numbers on my locker padlock until it clicks open.

"It's only a matter of time before we're back together and he puts you in your place."

I pull my books out of my locker one by one and put them into my bag.

"I'm talking to you." Vicki shoves my shoulder.

"And I'm ignoring you." I slide the last book in and close the locker door. "Goodbye, Vicki."

Turning away, I walk down the hallway. I might look confident on the outside, but inside I want to crawl into a hole because people are looking.

"This isn't over," she yells.

Shaking my head, I make my way out to my car and throw my bag into the back seat before sliding into the front. For a moment, I close my eyes and take a deep breath.

This part of my life is over.

I never have to set foot in this place ever again.

And now I get to take two months off and relax in the summer sun before getting back into studying again.

My eyes fly open as the passenger door opens and Patrick slips into the seat, sliding down below the windscreen.

"What are you doing?" I side-eye him.

"Hiding from Vicki. Quick, let's get out of here." He shoots me a cheeky smile, and I'm frozen for a moment.

I start the car just as Vicki appears at the gate.

"You owe me," I grumble.

Patrick chuckles as I pull out onto the street and drive in the direction of home.

"She's been trying to talk to me for days, and I'm so done."

"Really?" I stop at a red light.

"You don't believe me?"

I shrug. "You were together a long time."

He's quiet for a moment. The light changes to green. "It took me a long time to realise how shallow my life was. I want more."

Swallowing hard, I make the final turn into our street and pull into my driveway.

"Thanks."

I swear his dimples twinkle at me.

"You're welcome."

He runs his tongue over his upper lip. "What are you up to tomorrow night?"

I shrug. "Nothing that I know of."

"Want to catch a movie with me? We could go and get dinner first."

Swallowing hard, I drop my gaze. "I don't know."

He brushes his hand over mine. "Come on, Cassie. Give me a chance. I know I have a lot to make up for."

"It's just—"

"You don't trust me. Not yet."

I shrug again. "I don't know."

"Think about it? I'll come over in the morning and pester you about it."

I meet his gaze, and he grins at me again.

I can't help but smile. He's not going to give me an inch.

"Let me sleep on it."

Patrick nods slowly. "I can live with that. We have the whole summer. But I'll be on your doorstep first thing."

I laugh. "Whatever. Get out of here, Cross."

His eyes dance with amusement. "Roger that, Warren."

Once he's gone, I get out of the car, grab my bag from the back seat, and head inside.

"Cassie?" Mum calls from the kitchen. "Is that you?"

"It sure is."

I drop my bag at the base of the stairs and walk through to grab a drink.

"Was that Patrick getting out of your car?"

Laughing, I grab the juice out of the fridge and then pour a glass. "Can you see through walls?"

She smiles. "I might have been in the living room when you first got home."

I take a sip of my drink. "It was Patrick. He asked me to go to the movies with him tomorrow night."

. Mum claps her hands together. "Exciting. What about that girl he was seeing?"

"Oh they're finished." I gulp down the rest of the juice before putting the bottle back in the fridge. "She was right there today and he ignored her while he talked to me. It's just ..."

"You're worried he's not being honest with you."

I nod. When we were fifteen, one of Patrick's friends, Dave, asked me out. The whole thing was a prank. When we got to the car park of the cafe we were going to, he and his friends egged me. They called it a practical joke, but I ended up walking home in the hot sun and having the hassle of trying to get cooked egg out of my hair.

"Honey, he wasn't a part of that. And I don't think he'd hurt you like that."

Blowing out a long breath, I drop my gaze to my feet. "They were still friends. I don't want to feel this way, but ..."

"It's understandable."

"He says he wants a fresh start."

She gives my forearm a squeeze. "You two used to be close. Maybe you could be again."

"I told him I'd think about it tonight."

"Well, I think you should give him a chance. But it's obviously up to you."

"Thanks, Mum."

She pecks me on the cheek. "Love you. Now go and put your bag and books upstairs and then you can help me with dinner."

"Sure thing."

I skip up the stairs with an extra spring in my step.

Whether to let Patrick back into my life or not is a big decision.

But I have a feeling I know what I have to do.

4

CASSIE

Bright light peeps through a gap in the curtain and penetrates my closed eyelids.

Patrick wants his answer today.

And I've already decided to say yes.

He effectively dumped me as a friend five years ago, but he was never one of the bullies. I wish he'd done more to stop it—I'll be talking to him about that, but he seems genuine.

Our parents aren't close, but I don't think he'd risk upsetting mine or his.

It might be scary, but I want to take a chance.

"Cassie. Patrick is at the door." Mum's voice floats up the stairs.

"Give me a minute."

I strip out of my pyjamas and pull on jeans before slipping on a bra and T-shirt. Nerves make my stomach flutter, and I take a deep breath.

As I make my way down the stairs, Mum's voice still carries. It's been a long time since Patrick was over at my place—I'm sure she hasn't really spoken to him in years.

His eyes drift over to me, and he smiles.

"Hi," he says.

Sweat glistens on his biceps, bare in the tank top he's wearing. He runs—I've seen him. It's hard not to stare. His smile widens.

"I'll leave you two to it," Mum says. "It's good to see you, Patrick."

"You too, Mrs Warren."

Mum winks at me as she turns and heads toward the kitchen.

"I wondered if you were ready to go out with me tonight," Patrick says.

I rub the back of my neck. "I've just woken up."

His dimples pop when he grins. "You had all night. Please put me out of my misery."

I shrug. "Any girl from school would go out with you."

"Except the one I want." He reaches for my hands and takes them in his. "Come on, Cassie."

Pausing for a moment, I take another deep breath. "Okay. But anything mean and I'm not speaking to you ever again."

His eyes search mine. "I'd never hurt you on purpose. Pick you up about six? We'll go and get dinner and see a movie if that works for you."

Despite my wariness, I smile. "That sounds great."

He beams. "Great. See you then."

Dropping my hands, he then turns and jogs across the road to his house.

After closing the door, I make my way into the kitchen. The newspaper's laid out on the dining room table, and Dad's poring over it, a steaming cup of coffee in his hands.

"So?" Mum asks.

"Tonight at six. Dinner and a movie."

Dad raises his head. "Have you got a date?"

I nod. "With Patrick Cross."

He smiles. "So, you're going out with the school rugby captain."

I laugh. Like a lot of kiwi men, he loves his rugby. It's not surprising that this is how he thinks. "I am."

"As long as he treats you right. That's all I ask. You're old enough to make your own decisions now."

"That means he trusts you not to go out and get pregnant," Mum translates.

"Dad! It's *one* date. I'm not having sex with him."

"I'd rather not think about that at all." He chuckles and goes back to his newspaper.

My face burns, while Mum wraps an arm around my waist. "We trust you."

"It's one date, and we haven't even gone on it yet."

"It's best to be prepared."

I roll my eyes and leave the room. In the hallway, I punch the air and mount the stairs two at a time. While I'm sure things won't go that far, it will be nice if he kisses me.

When we were eleven, Patrick leaned in to kiss my cheek right as I turned my head and our lips met. We stared at each other for a moment before blushing and going our separate ways. By the end of the following year, our friendship had faded.

I've missed the ease between us, but maybe today is a fresh start.

BY QUARTER TO SIX, I'm showered and dressed—a light summer dress as the weather's already hot and I'm worried I'll be a pool of sweat with anxiety, let alone the heat.

My long, auburn hair's scooped back into a ponytail to keep it off my face, and I kept my make-up light but used Mum's vanilla perfume.

Her scent is warm and comforting, and I'm hoping it'll help me get through this nerve-racking first date.

"You look gorgeous, love," Dad says.

"Thanks, Dad."

My heart beats out of my chest when a tap on the door tells me Patrick's here.

Mum gives my hand a squeeze and lets go so I can answer it.

"Hey." He beams a bright smile at me when I open the door.

I swallow hard and nod. "Hi."

"Ready? I thought we might check out that new burger place in town. It's not a long walk to the movie theatre, and it's a nice night."

I nod. "That sounds great."

"You look beautiful."

Oh my God.

I never thought I'd hear those words out of Patrick's mouth not once, but twice, and I blink rapidly to stop tears building up. Coming from Dad is one thing. But Patrick?

"Thank you."

He leads me out to his car and opens the passenger door for me. It seems like he's really going all out for this.

Tension rolls out of my shoulders as my anxiety level drops.

Patrick gets into the car and smiles at me. "Ready?"

I nod.

"I'm so glad you agreed to come out with me. This is a fresh start for us."

I can't help but smile. "I agree."

"Good. I've missed you." He reaches across and takes my hand in his. "I'm sorry I've been such a dickhead."

For a moment, I can't quite believe my ears, but then I laugh. "As long as you know."

His eyes sparkle with mischief. "I do." He gives my hand a squeeze. "Let's go."

It's not a long drive, but I spend the whole ride watching the scenery go by out the window. My heart's still pounding so hard, I'm afraid to look at Patrick and find that this is all a dream.

When we pull into a car park, he turns to me.

"Stay right there. I'll get the door."

My cheeks are flush with excitement.

He opens the door and holds out his hand for me to take.

This is it.

People will see us together—maybe even people we went to school with. I'm nervous, but proud, and trying to ignore the sinking feeling in my gut.

He doesn't let go as he leads me through the door.

I lock gazes with Dave Pratt.

Patrick must see him too, as he squeezes my hand.

"Ignore him. Tell me what you want and I'll order it. You find a seat."

"Just a cheeseburger."

He cocks his head. "I'm paying. Have whatever you want. I seem to remember you were partial to fries."

I smile. "You have a better memory than I ever gave you credit for."

Leaning forward, he whispers in my ear, "There are those dimples again. They get me every time."

I laugh and slap his forearm gently. "Where have you been?"

"With my head up my arse. I don't know, but it wasn't the right place." He sighs.

"I'll find a seat."

He places a kiss on my nose, and I laugh as he walks toward the counter.

Turning, I take a look around before my eyes land on an empty table. It's right by the wall and there's no one else close.

Perfect.

I make my way over to it and drop into the seat. My stomach flutters, and I'm not sure if it's hunger or nerves. This change in Patrick is still so hard to believe.

Casting my gaze around the room, I lock eyes with Dave again. He gives me a blank look, and I turn my back on him to avoid seeing him again.

"Are you alright?" Patrick's voice comes from behind me, and I shuffle on my chair to face him as he sits down with a tray of food.

"I'm fine."

He nods in the direction of Dave. "I punched him in the

face when he hurt you."

"What?" My heart thuds, but questions swirl in my mind and I can't let go.

"I tried to stop any bullying. If anyone's said anything bad since then—I'm sorry. I made it clear to everyone I knew that you were out of bounds. I'm sure they haven't always done as I ask though, and that pisses me off."

"Really?" I search his eyes for any sign that he's making this up, but he's so earnest.

"Really. I also had a chat with Dave about what happened and got to the bottom of it. I'm so sorry for everything."

I draw in a deep breath. "It's not always been good, but I appreciate the effort." After picking up a fry from the tray, I chew on it for a moment and swallow. "So, tell me again why you never asked me out before?"

He chuckles. "I had a girlfriend. One I was with for way too long. And then there was the fact that you always made me nervous, you're so smart. I never thought you'd be interested in me in that way."

Are you kidding?

"Why not?"

Patrick shrugs. "I guess I've been an idiot."

"Yeah. You have."

Our meal is peppered with conversation. For two people who were once so close, we're like strangers catching up with each other's lives.

But it's also like slipping on an old pair of shoes.

He's comfortable to be around, even if he makes my heart race.

Once we've finished eating, Patrick holds my hand all the

way to the movie theatre. No one's looking at us, but I feel seen for the first time in my life.

We cast our gazes over the movie posters inside the door.

"Which movie did you want to see? The new Marvel movie's out, but there's also a rom-com that looks pretty good," he says.

"Do you really want to watch a rom-com?" I tilt my head and smile.

"I would if you wanted to see it. But I'll leave the choice up to you." He squeezes my hand, and I blow out a long breath.

"Marvel any day of the week."

He chuckles. "Oh thank God."

Leading me to the ticket queue, he holds my hand tight. I can't remember a time when I've been so happy—at least not in the past few years.

I've got my best friend back.

Even if nothing comes of this, the pressure that's been sitting on my chest every time I saw him these past few years has lessened.

And every time he does something sweet, my guard lowers a little more.

"Popcorn?" he asks.

"Yes, please."

I bounce on the balls of my heels while he buys tickets and snacks. It's been a long time since I've been to a movie theatre—I'd rather watch a movie at home or read a book, but I am looking forward to this.

It's different when you're not alone.

I follow him into the theatre once he's got everything.

I could get used to this.

"Let's sit up the back," Patrick says.

We're still early enough to get good seats, and as the theatre fills up, nerves keep eating at my stomach.

Will he kiss me?

Am I overthinking everything?

The lights dim, and the trailers start. Patrick laces his fingers with mine and smiles when I meet his gaze.

I like this.

I like *him*.

I always did.

When the movie starts, he squeezes my fingers tight and leans toward me. I meet him in the middle and rest my head on his shoulder.

He feels safe.

As the movie goes on, I'm acutely aware of him—his clean, soapy smell, the way his breathing's so steady when mine is a mess being so close to him.

"Cassie," he murmurs in my ear.

Even in the darkened theatre, everything he needs to say shows in his eyes. They study my features, and I hold my breath when he licks his lips.

A lump forms in my throat as every nerve in my body tingles. He leans closer, grazing my lips with his before he presses down, kissing me gently.

"Patrick," I whisper.

He kisses me again, and this time he slips his tongue between my lips. At first, I'm taken aback, but I lean into it, tasting him for the first time.

I wish I knew what I was doing.

When the kiss ends, he keeps his gaze focused on mine before reaching up to cup my cheek. My breath quickens, his expression so soft and tender. No one's ever looked at me like this before—and I close my eyes as he presses his forehead to mine for a moment.

The rest of the movie is a blur, and as he takes my hand again and leads me out of the theatre, warmth blossoms in my chest. This isn't a prank.

This is real.

Watching the credits roll at the end, I snuggle up to his side, and he plants a soft kiss in my hair before he holds my hand all the way out to the street.

"That was awesome. I've been wanting to see that for a while," he says.

I grin. "I loved it."

"Although …" He comes to a stop in front of his car and turns toward me. "I was distracted for quite a lot of it."

I laugh as he slides his arms around my waist. "Me too."

Patrick kisses me softly. "Let's get you home."

He lingers before letting me go and walks to the other side of the car to open my door.

"Thank you," I say.

"You're welcome."

I climb in and buckle up my seatbelt as he gets in the driver's side.

My chest is bursting with happiness—he really does like me.

He's being all gentlemanly, but I'm not ready for this night to end.

"At least now we're on holiday, we can see each other every day," he says as he starts the car.

"I'd like that."

He drives me home and all the while, the way he kissed

me plays over and over again in my brain. I always wanted him to be the one, but I never thought I stood a chance.

Now what happens?

The possibilities make me giddy.

When he pulls his car into my driveway, I already feel lost. It's insane. We went without each other for years, but it's the way it was when we were kids—wanting to spend all our time together.

He opens my car door and walks with me to the door.

"Thank you for tonight. It was great."

"It was." My cheeks flush.

"See you tomorrow?"

"I hope so."

He lowers his head and kisses me again. "Goodnight, Cassie."

"Goodnight," I whisper.

Patrick waits in his car until I'm inside—despite living right across the road.

I close the door behind me, hope building in my chest.

"Was that Patrick kissing you?"

Mum's voice behind me wakes me out of my thoughts, and I laugh. "Were you watching?"

She gives me a soft smile. "I might have been. It's nice to see you happy. It's been a long time coming."

I hug her tight. "I'm going to bed."

"Not going to stay up and tell us everything?"

Rolling my eyes, I let her go and head toward the stairs. "Goodnight."

She laughs as I take the stairs two at a time, running until I reach my bedroom window. Patrick's out of his car and standing in the light of the front door as he looks up at my room. He waves and blows me a kiss.

I'm never going to get any sleep.

Patrick proved to me tonight that I can trust him with my feelings.

The only lingering doubt is what happens if Patrick's friends don't accept we're together? He's been with Vicki so long, and she's a part of that clique.

I just hope that he sides with me if it comes to that.

5

PATRICK

I can't believe how dumb I've been.

Cassie was my everything at one point in my life. Granted, we were much younger, but how did I ever waver from that path?

She pulled away first. I'm not sure if she realised she was doing it. Once we started high school and the time I spent on other interests grew, she buried her nose in books. I don't resent her—she was always the smarter one out of the two of us.

And at fifteen, I met Vicki. I mean, she was always there, at school, but when it was clear I was destined to be captain of the rugby team—the only thing that seemed to matter to the school as much as academic prowess—she showed interest in me.

For a while, I was lost in the long legs and blonde hair. But time showed me another side to Vicki. With me she was bright, bubbly, friendly. The flip side to that was the bitchiness, the cliquey behaviour, the gossip.

I hated that. I just wanted to get on with school and sport.

It took me by surprise to find out that Cassie had a date with Dave. We were so distant at that point, we might as well have been in different countries. Vicki and I were supposed to go out that night but she told me she wasn't feeling well, and I stayed in and watched a movie instead.

That was the first time we really fought.

Mum and Dad weren't happy to find out I punched Dave until I told them what he'd done to Cassie. Mum always harboured dreams of us ending up together, but even then I couldn't see how she'd ever agree to be friends after the way my other friends had treated her.

It wasn't until I saw her that night at the dance, her long auburn hair flowing behind her in that cream-coloured dress that I realised just how badly I wanted to be back in her life. She looked free and unburdened of the stress she always seemed to carry around on her back—always working hard to achieve the results she wanted.

She was beautiful—is beautiful.

"You're home early," Mum says as I walk into the living room.

"The movie finished, so I'm home." I shoot her the side eye, unsure why she thinks this. I've never been a big party-goer, and I took school seriously enough to be home reasonably early most nights.

"Yes, but you were on a date."

"I know."

She rolls her eyes at me, and Dad just chuckles.

"Want a coffee?" he asks.

"That'd be great, Dad."

He grabs Mum's mug and heads into the kitchen while I flop onto the couch.

Mum smiles at me. "So, how did it go?"

"Well …" I knew she'd be digging. "We had burgers and then went to a movie. The movie was great."

"You know that's not what I'm asking." She narrows her eyes at me.

"I know." I laugh. "It was good, Mum. Cassie had a good time."

"It's good to see you two together."

I nod. "I messed up for way too long. But I'm fixing it."

She sighs. "It's about time. I'm glad it's happened before we move. Is she still going to Auckland Uni?"

"Yep. We haven't talked much about that yet, but she told me she is."

"Be careful with her heart, Patrick. She's not Vicki."

"I know she's not."

"I like her. Cassie was always such a sweet girl."

I fix my gaze on my mother's. "She still is. We're dating, Mum. I figure we have the summer to work out where this is heading."

She nods. "Just be careful. And watch Vicki because you know she'll try and cause trouble."

"I know. And I'll be keeping a close eye on everything. I don't trust Vicki anywhere near Cassie."

Clearly I've said the right thing, as she smiles. I love my mother, and I love how protective she is over Cassie. We've clashed in the past as she didn't believe I was doing enough for her, and I was so far in my head, I thought everything was as it should be.

It's obvious now that things haven't been right for a very long time, and that's entirely on me.

But now I have the summer to make things right and get Cassie and me back on track.

Auckland can be the fresh start we need.

———

I'M on her doorstep the following morning.

Not so early this time—I was always the early bird while she likes her sleep.

Cassie's mother smiles when she opens the door. "She's just having coffee. Come in."

It's the first time in years I've been in this house, but it's as familiar to me as my own.

I walk through to the kitchen. Cassie's at the dining table with her father, and she looks up, her eyes widening.

I told you I'd be here.

"Morning, Patrick," Mr Warren says.

"Good morning." I smile.

"Hey," Cassie says.

I take a seat next to her. "I thought we could go for a walk on the beach. Maybe grab some lunch later?"

She shoots me a shy smile over her coffee cup, and it makes my heart clench.

I want to be with her—only her.

It messes with my head to think I could have had this all along.

"I'd like that."

"It's nearly ten now, so I thought maybe we could go for a drive around first and head over to Napier."

Her smile widens. "I'll just finish this and grab my bag."

"No rush."

"Looking forward to Auckland?" Mr Warren asks.

I nod. "I can't wait. Mum and Dad got a house in a great spot—not too far from the university."

"That's good. I can't bear the thought of living in the big smoke. But if you can make it work." He chuckles.

"It'll be different. I'll miss this place. Never thought we'd all be moving, but things just worked out that way."

"And you'll be near Cassie." His gaze pierces me.

"Ready to go?" Cassie interrupts.

"Sure."

She stands and grabs my hand, pulling me toward the door.

"See you later, Dad," she calls over her shoulder.

I wait at the base of the stairs as she runs up to get her bag.

She rolls her eyes as she runs back down, grabbing my hand again and pulling me out the front door.

"I am so, so sorry," she says. "I was sure he was about to ask you what your intentions are."

I laugh. "Oh, I'm not sure he'd like the answer to that."

I click the key fob to the car to unlock it, and she goes to the passenger side while I get into the driver's seat.

"Why wouldn't he like the answer?" she asks.

"Because I'm not sure any parent would be a fan of my intentions toward you." I reach over and give her knee a squeeze.

She swallows hard.

Leaning over, I give her a soft kiss on the lips. "You're all mine for the day. Let's get out of here."

Cassie's smile warms my heart.

———

AT THE BEACH, the hot sun beats down on us, and despite the sun block, my skin feels like it's on fire.

In front of us, a girl in a bikini drops a towel to the ground before she looks toward us. She's tall, brunette, and looks vaguely familiar—I think we went to school with her. Her face lights up and she waves in our direction.

Cassie's grip on my hand slackens, and I shift my gaze to her. Her head is bowed, and the smile's gone from her face.

"Cass? You okay?" I come to a stop and pull her into my arms.

For a second, she protests, but she rolls her eyes and lets me slip my arms around her waist.

"Why are you with me?"

"What do you mean? You know why. I want to spend time with you—see where this goes."

"But you could have anyone."

She won't meet my gaze.

"I want you."

Cassie raises her face until her eyes meet mine. She's still not smiling, and I hate it.

"Patrick—"

"I mean it. You're what I want. Not another Vicki. You're beautiful, smart, and I can have an actual conversation with you that doesn't deteriorate into gossip."

She snorts, before pulling away from me and slapping her hand over her nose.

"And you have a sense of humour. We used to laugh all the time, remember?"

"I thought you'd be more interested in someone like Vicki." She nods toward the bikini-clad girl. "Someone like her."

"What? Why?"

She waves her hands down her body. Cassie's a classic hourglass shape. She's busty with hips, and the jeans she's wearing fit her snugly.

"I'm with you because I want you. Not her. Not anyone else. *You.*"

Her cheeks flush. "What are you doing to me, Patrick Cross?" she asks.

"Something I should have done a long time ago. Trying to make things right with us."

She smiles. There's something special about Cassie's smile—there always was. Whenever I was down about school or sport or anything else, all I had to do is spend a bit of time in the warmth of that smile and it made everything right.

How did I ever forget that?

"I didn't know if I could trust you at first," she whispers, and a little piece of me curls up and dies inside.

"I hope I'm proving you can."

"You're doing all the right things." She shares that smile with me again, and my throat tightens.

She's so down to earth and, well, normal. There's no bitchiness or gossip. She's just Cassie.

My Cassie.

And she is my Cassie, whether she's fully aware of it or not.

My heart feels more full than it has in a long time.

6

CASSIE

Falling in love makes it the best summer of my life.

The time flies by, and before I know it, the end of summer approaches.

Patrick and his parents will soon be moving to Auckland. The moving truck's booked, but his parents decided to head down to Wellington for the weekend for his father's school reunion.

So, Patrick has the house all to himself for a couple of days.

His parents have also agreed that he can have a farewell party in a couple of weeks when they've got another weekend away before they move.

The thought of it makes me nervous. While there are certain people we both agreed wouldn't be on the guest list, there'll still be people there who never bothered with me at school. And even though we've spent all summer together, being seen in public, with Patrick being very affectionate at times, I'm not sure what they'll think of us as a couple.

Patrick doesn't care. But then he's not the one who was bullied in school.

"I thought I might make us dinner tonight," Patrick says.

"Can you even cook?" I poke my tongue at him, and he laughs.

"I'm pretty sure I can make steak and salad." Patrick leans back on the couch. "We've got to get through what's in the freezer, and I know how to cook steak."

I smile. "Sounds good."

"Stay with me tonight."

I search his eyes for some sign of how far he wants to go with this.

"I can't stay all night. My parents will kill me."

He takes my hand in his. "I want to be with you, Cassie. We've got the house to ourselves, and I thought after dinner we could …" He swallows hard. "Go to bed together."

My eyes widen. "You want to have sex?"

"Only if you want to."

My heart's racing. "I want to be with you. You know I haven't done it before, right?"

His soft smile melts my heart. "Neither have I."

"Really? I thought you and Vicki …"

He shakes his head. "No. She wanted to, but I wasn't ready. I think I was waiting for you. I just didn't know it at the time."

Biting my bottom lip, I nod. "I want this. I want you."

"I'm sure we can work it out together."

He leans over and kisses me, deepening the kiss after a moment, his hand resting just below my breast.

Tingles shoot up my spine—they always do when he kisses me. But this time, it's different.

This is forever.

I'm so in love with Patrick Cross—I thought I was before, but that was nothing like I feel now.

"I'll get cooking." He gives my hand a squeeze, and I sit at the dining table while he hustles around the kitchen.

It doesn't take long for things to be sizzling away, but I bite my tongue as he flips the steak over and over trying to get it to brown.

"I'm not sure about your cooking skills."

He laughs. "I've never been good at it. Mum despairs because she says I'm incapable of learning. I'm not sure if that's true, but I wanted to do this for you."

I wrap my arms around him from behind. "You're a good boyfriend, you know?"

"I hope so."

"You are."

He lets go of the pan and turns toward me. "I love you, Cassie."

My heart seizes. It thuds so hard I can hear it in my head. "I love you too."

The pan sizzles. I wrinkle my nose as a burning smell wafts across the room.

"Oh, shit," he cries.

I'm the worst girlfriend in the world when I laugh and back away.

He turns off the element and pulls the pan from the heat. "I guess it's time to eat."

"Are you sure it's safe?"

His eyes narrow. "I'll make you pay for that."

"I'm sure you will."

He nods toward the dining table. "Go and take a seat and I'll serve this up."

I do as he asks and smile as he places a plate in front of me. It doesn't look too bad, but the steak is a little scorched. If it were barbecue, it'd look perfect.

He sits across from me.

I pick up my knife and fork and make the first cut—at least I try to. I can't meet his gaze as, even with a steak knife, I have to slide the knife back and forward until I cut a slice.

He watches as I raise it to my mouth and slip it in.

And then I chew. And chew. It takes a while, but finally I've chewed it enough to swallow. "You know, this isn't too bad. Just a little tough."

He snorts. "It's not great. You don't have to pretend."

"But it's made with love." I flutter my eyelashes at him before laughing and soon he's joining in.

"So, pizza?"

I place my hand on my heart. "I thought you'd never ask."

His eyes grow sad, and he lets out a sigh. "I'm so sorry, Cassie. I wanted tonight to be perfect."

"It is."

Patrick's eyebrows rise.

"No, it really is," I say. "The only thing that matters is that we're here together. That's all. Maybe next time I can cook for you."

His lips twitch into a smile. "Do you remember when you entered that baking competition and won with that chocolate cake you made? And then we took off with it and ate the whole thing between us?"

"We were ten."

He laughs. "You were always better at that kind of thing than me. I had two left hands."

"Maybe I can teach you to cook."

"Maybe when we move in together."

I laugh. "And when will that be?"

He shrugs. "When we're ready."

"You're that confident this is going to work?"

Patrick cocks an eyebrow. "Between us? We're forever, babe."

I stand and pick up my plate. "Well until that happens, how about I take care of this while you order a pizza?"

"I can clean up."

"No, I'll sort this out. You did your best, and I appreciate it."

As I make my way around the table to collect his plate, he grabs me by the hips and pulls me onto his lap. "You're a good girlfriend. The best."

"I hope so." I lean my head against his before standing again and picking up his plate.

With it only being the two of us, it doesn't take long to scrape the plates into the bin and place them in the dishwasher.

"Pizza will be here in about twenty minutes."

I slide my arms around his neck. "Thank you."

"For what? I haven't even managed to feed you yet."

I laugh. "For being you. For trying. I bet you never did this for anyone else before."

He places his hands on my hips. "I never wanted to before."

I sigh as he kisses me, and then I'm lost in the man I love. Closing my eyes, I let out a moan as he deepens the kiss, his tongue dancing with mine as his hands slip around to cup my arse.

When he lets me up for air, he presses his forehead to mine. "How am I supposed to wait through dinner after that?"

He tugs me closer, and my heart speeds up, feeling him hard against me.

"I..."

"It's okay. Give me a minute." He drops his lips to below my ear and places a gentle kiss there. "I need to calm down and wait."

"I'll go and sit on the couch."

"That would probably be a good idea."

I pop a kiss on his nose. "I'll give you a minute."

Chills run through me as I make my way to the couch. *I did that to Patrick?* I'd suspected it at times during heavy make-out sessions, but he's been such a gentleman he's never pushed, and I'm probably a bit oblivious to these things, never having had a boyfriend before.

A few minutes later, he joins me on the couch but keeps a bit of distance between us. I get it. The last thing he needs when opening the door to the pizza delivery is an erection.

Besides, I think he's a little embarrassed.

Maybe we are having sex tonight, but if he's anything like me he won't want to talk about it until we're in his bedroom. I don't have the confidence to speak up.

A knock on the front door makes us both jump.

He laughs. "This is so awkward and I'm sorry. We can just eat the pizza and call it a night if you want. Maybe watch a movie?"

"That's not what I want."

Patrick nods then goes the door and brings back the pizza.

"I don't want that either, but I don't want to push you."

"You're not. I'm ready." I give him what I hope is a confident smile.

"Let's eat, then."

He places the pizza on the coffee table and opens the box.

I burst out laughing. It's half meat lovers—his favourite—and half chicken—mine.

"Much better than that awful steak." He picks up a piece, the cheese stretching as he wraps it around the end of the slice.

I grab a slice of the chicken. "You'll get better at it. Give it time. We should have used the barbecue."

Patrick snickers. "I should have thought of that in the first place."

Taking a bite, I let out a long moan. "Oh God, this is so good."

"Cass, you're not supposed to make me hard until I'm ready for it."

I stare at him. "What do you mean?"

"The way you moaned over that piece of pizza. I'm not sure I can handle that."

I laugh, and it eases the tension in me. I'm terrified at the idea of having sex, but I want to. I want to be with Patrick. I want him to be my first and my only.

It makes me feel better that we'll be experiencing this for the first time together. Maybe it would help if one of us knew what we were doing, but we're smart enough to work it out.

All I know is that I really do love him.

7

CASSIE

My legs are shaking as I make my way up the stairs to Patrick's room.

So many things are churning around in my head.

I know he'll understand if I change my mind. I know he'll be patient because it's just who he is.

Even if we get things wrong, we'll be together.

"So, this is my bedroom." He's so cute when he's flustered.

"I've only been in here about a million times." I look around. Nothing's changed too much in here. When we were kids, he had posters of comic book characters and they're gone. But the room is still decorated the same, and he has all the same furniture except for the bed.

He used to have a single bed on the corner, and now he's got a queen size.

I sit on the side of the bed. Patrick walks toward me until he's standing between my thighs, his hands cupping my face.

"Whatever happens, I want you to know that any time if you change your mind, we'll stop."

I nod. "That goes for you too."

"I'm not changing my mind. This has been in my head all summer. I love you, and you drive me crazy. And I want everything with you." He steps back and slips his shirt over his head.

All I can do is stare.

"Hang on a minute." He switches on the lamp beside the bed and walks over to the door, turning off the light. "That's better. More romantic."

He moves closer again. He's so cut, his abdominal muscles firmly defined. I reach out and place my palms against them.

"I like your hands on me," he murmurs.

"I want to touch you."

"How about we get undressed?"

My head shoots up and I meet his gaze. "Uhh I …"

"I want to see you too."

I rise to my feet. My heart pounding, I lift my shirt over my head.

"Oh, God," he whispers, his eyes fixed on my breasts.

Confidence growing, I reach behind me and undo my bra. I drop it to the floor.

Patrick's tongue darts out and slides across his lips.

It's all I need to know he's not going to freak out at me.

"I want to touch you," he says.

"Then do it."

He cups my breasts in his hands and runs his thumbs across my nipples.

"You're even more perfect that I could ever have imagined."

My breath quickens, and before I chicken out, I unbutton my jeans and push them down.

Patrick moves back and runs his gaze down as I slip my jeans and underwear off.

"Cassie?"

"Yes," I whisper.

"Lie on the bed. I really want to see your pussy."

My cheeks flush, but I pull back the top sheet and lie down. Patrick's gaze is fixed on mine, and then he runs it down my body, his chest heaving.

He pushes off his jeans, and my eyes widen. I've seen pictures of cocks in biology, but his is long and thick and very hard.

I bite my bottom lip.

"You have to stop looking at me like that." He smirks.

"It's just … I …"

He rounds the bed and lies down beside me, pulling me into his arms. My body reacts to the feel of us skin to skin.

My breasts feel heavy. My pussy clenches.

Patrick kisses me long and deep, running his hand down my side.

"You okay?"

I nod. "I like the way you look at me."

"I like looking at you."

My breath hitches as his mouth closes over one nipple, his hand on my other breast caressing.

"Oh," I squeak.

He raises his head. "You like that?"

"I like it very much."

His attention returns to my breast, and I arch my back, eager for more.

He trails his fingers over my stomach—I flinch, but Patrick kisses my nipple and meets my gaze.

"You don't have to be scared."

"You're just so … perfect. And I'm—"

"Beautiful, you're beautiful. I want all of this, Cass. I want *you.*"

His hand drifts down past my hips, and his eyes never leave mine as I guide his fingers to my clit.

"Cassie," he whispers.

"I love you." I cup his cheek with my free hand. "I've always loved you."

I close my eyes briefly as he slides his fingers back and forward.

"I'm sorry I—"

"We're not talking about that. Not now." I open my eyes and gaze into his. "This is all that matters."

He nods, bending his head to kiss me again.

His fingers continue to work me, and he sucks in a breath as he slips them inside me for the first time.

"You're so wet. Can I …" His eyes search mine. "Can I go down on you?"

"I think I'd like that."

My cheeks heat up as I spread my legs and he moves between them, his gaze sweeping over my body. I've never been so vulnerable for anyone before.

"Patrick?"

His eyes search mine. "Yes?"

"I'm glad it's you."

He smiles. "Me too. I can be myself with you."

Slowly he moves, and I freeze when his hot breath hits my upper thigh. He places gentle kisses on my skin, and I relax again.

"You smell so good." He leans tentatively forward, prying me open with his fingers.

He licks me before finding my clit with his tongue and teasing it. I gasp, and he raises his head. "Is that good?"

"So good."

His smile is hesitant, but he goes back to it, and this time between his lips and his fingers, I don't just start to take off— I soar.

"Oh my God."

I shudder, pleasure taking over my body, and Patrick gets up on his knees. "I did that. I made you come."

"Yeah, you did." I'm breathless. I've brought myself to orgasm before, but it's so much better when he does it. The look of wonder on his face makes my cheeks flush.

"I think we're ready. Do you want to help me put the condom on?"

I nod rapidly. At least I know how to do that—those biology classes with Mrs Nixon are about to come in handy.

He reaches into his side cabinet and pulls out a box.

I'm breathing so heavily I'm scared I'll hyperventilate.

Patrick smiles at me as he pulls out a foiled packet.

I push myself up to sit, take it from him with shaky hands, and tear it open.

He moves closer.

I pinch the end of the condom and roll it down his cock. He's so warm and hard, and his breathing grows erratic as I do it.

"I love you touching me," he murmurs.

Lying back down, I spread my legs wider. His eyes drink me in.

"Are you ready?" he asks.

"I want you. I want everything with you."

He settles his weight over me, and I rest one hand on his pecs. I reach down with the other to guide him.

With a push of his hips, he slides inside me and moans. "Oh, damn. You feel so good. Are you okay?"

I nod, heat rising in my cheeks. I've never felt so open and vulnerable. This is perfect—Patrick's made it perfect.

"I'm just going to stop for a second. Give you a chance to get used to it."

His eyes meet mine.

This summer has been the best season of my life. I thought I loved him before, but now I'm in love with him and it's the best feeling in the world.

He kisses me, soft and sweet as he starts to thrust slowly.

"I'm not sure I'll last long this first time."

"We'd better get lots of practice, then." I smile, and he chuckles, the vibration shooting through my body.

"That works for me."

I do my best to keep my breathing steady, but the pinch that happened when he first started moving inside me subsides and my eyelids flutter as I fight to keep my eyes open.

"Patrick," I whisper.

He trails kisses down my neck until he reaches my breasts, sucking lightly on one nipple.

"I can't believe you're mine," he says. "All mine."

"I am." I run my hands up his spine. "And you're mine."

I bring my hips up to match him, and we find a rhythm.

Tension shows in his face, his gaze locking with mine. We rise together and then we fall, and he lets out a groan, his body stiffening against mine.

"Oh my God," he says. His breathing's heavy, and he comes to a stop.

We lie there for a moment, basking in the afterglow before he slowly lifts his weight and moves to my side.

"I have to get rid of this and then I'll be back. Okay?"

I nod. "Okay."

When he's gone, self-consciousness creeps over me, and I pull the blanket up to cover me.

Patrick smiles as he walks back to the bed and climbs in beside me.

He nuzzles the nape of my neck. "I know I asked before, but are you okay?"

"So much better than okay."

His hot breath tickles my shoulders when he laughs. "I really do love you, Cassie. I'm so glad we found each other like this."

"Me too." I sigh. "I should go."

"Stay a bit longer. Just lie with me a while."

I shouldn't, but I close my eyes. I'm so safe and warm in his arms, and I never want to leave his bed.

And before I know it, sleep pulls at me until I'm gone.

I'm so hot.

My eyelids don't want to open, but I force them to.

It takes a moment for me to remember where I am.

Patrick's wrapped around me, his heavy thigh resting over mine. We're both hot and sticky from the summer heat —the humidity must have risen while were sleeping.

I look around for a clock, but most of Patrick's things went with the movers.

Shoving his leg off mine, I reach over him to where his phone is on the bedside cabinet. Mine's still in my bag somewhere downstairs.

"What's going on?"

"I just need to check the time."

"It's still early," he mumbles, but his eyes are closed and he's moving like a sloth—still half asleep.

Pressing the power button on his phone lights up the screen.

2:07 a.m.

"Oh my God. I didn't mean to fall asleep. My parents are going to kill me." I drop his phone back on the cabinet and pull away.

Patrick laughs as I scramble out of bed and drag my underwear on.

"They know where you are. If they were angry, they'd be here."

"That's not the point."

He rests his hand on my spine. "I should have set an alarm. I'm sorry."

"No, it's my fault too. I shouldn't have closed my eyes." I pull my shirt over my head and turn round to face him. "Your bed was too comfortable."

He grins. "When we get our own place, we'll get a new bed together."

"I like that idea." I lean over and peck him on the lips.

"I love you. See you later?"

"I'll text you."

I curse myself all the way out of his house and across the road. All I can do is hope Mum and Dad have gone to sleep.

Maybe I'm eighteen now, but I think they'd be disappointed if I stayed out all night.

The house is quiet. I open the front door and make my way in. The kitchen light is on, and I groan.

Mum appears in the doorway. "Want a hot chocolate?"

I could just go to bed. But I get the feeling she wants to talk. Especially since she stayed up this late.

"Sounds good." I follow her back into the kitchen. "I didn't think you'd still be up."

She shrugs. "You might be an adult now and about to leave home, but I still worry. That's what you do when you're a parent."

"I'm sorry. I fell asleep."

Mum reaches for two mugs as the jug boils. "I'm just glad you're home."

I lean on the bench with my elbows. "I really am sorry, Mum. I didn't mean to stay out so late. We had dinner, and Patrick made a mess of it. So then we had pizza. And then during the evening I fell asleep when I didn't mean to. I just woke up and freaked out and thought it was better to come home than stay out all night."

"Like I said, I'm glad you're home."

She makes the hot chocolate in silence, and then we take it into the living room to drink it.

Mum studies me closely. "So you two are serious?"

I nod. "We are. Patrick keeps talking about getting a place together in Auckland."

Mum frowns. "I thought you were staying in the student accommodation."

"I am. But maybe not forever." I take a sip of hot chocolate.

She smiles. "I want you to be happy. And if being with him makes you happy, then I'm all for it. Just be careful, Cassie. You've got such a gentle heart and I don't want to see it hurt."

"I promise."

If only I realised just how empty that promise was.

8

CASSIE

In the two weeks since we first slept together, we've been inseparable.

We haven't had the opportunity to sneak anywhere to have sex again, but our relationship is at a whole other level.

I'm not sure what Auckland will bring, but we're together now and I hope we can move in together one day.

At least when we're at uni, I'll have a room of my own and Patrick can spend nights with me.

We can't wait.

My parents know what's going on—at least, my mother does. I'm not sure about Patrick's parents, but they're in the midst of packing the house to move and we never get a moment alone at either house.

But I'm content in a way I've never been.

I wish the years we weren't close hadn't happened, but now it's like old times—only better.

Patrick's parents are away tonight—most of the packing

is done and they've taken a trip to Wellington to see Patrick's grandparents. They'd given permission for Patrick to have the farewell party, although Patrick's been in two minds about having it now he no longer hangs out with the crowd he used to. But there are good people that he knew—people that he wants one chance to say goodbye to.

It's coincided with a promise I made to my father to help with the stocktake of the hardware store he works at. I'll get to the party late, but I'll be there, and I'm looking forward to the chance to let my hair down before Patrick moves.

It's the end of January, and while the Crosses move in a couple of days, there's still another month before I shift to Auckland. It's going to be the hardest month of my life.

By the time the stocktake is over, it's even later than I thought it'd be. I've texted Patrick with no response, but then he'll be surrounded by people and music and I'm not sure he'll hear his phone.

I walk through a house full of people from school. Dave Pratt watches me from across the room, and I frown. I didn't know he'd be here.

The music's thumping, but the party's not out of control which is a relief. I think his parents would kill him if it was.

There's no sign of him in the living room, or the kitchen, and a quick scan of the backyard doesn't give me any clue of where he is.

Until Kelly Banks comes bouncing into the kitchen.

Why the hell is she invited? She's Vicki's best friend.

Unease creeps up my spine.

"Are you looking for Patrick?" she asks.

I nod, unable to speak.

"He went up to his room. It was all a bit noisy for him."

None of this makes sense.

I climb the stairs, the pit in my stomach growing with each step. If it was too noisy, why didn't he send them all home?

Why is Kelly here?

Patrick's bedroom door is closed—all the doors up here are, presumably to keep people out of the rooms.

I draw in a deep breath before reaching for the door handle and turning.

The room is lit dimly—only the bedside lamp is on.

Blonde hair fans out from the pillow closest to me. My head swims.

I come to a halt, unable to believe the sight in front of me.

There's a kissing sound before the blonde sits up and smirks at me.

The beat of the music fades as blood rushes in my ears.

Vicki meets my gaze, the sheet pulled up over her bare breasts. "Oh. I didn't think *you* were invited."

"Patrick?" I croak.

He raises his head. His eyes are glazed over—he's been drinking, but that's no excuse.

"Cassie." He flashes a lazy smile before putting his head back down.

She rubs his back. "It's okay. I'll take care of it."

Meeting my gaze, she shoots me a look so cold that I shiver. "Get out, Cassie. He got what he wanted and now he's mine again."

"What did you do?"

"We all bet he couldn't convince you to have sex with him. It didn't take him anywhere near as long as I thought it would—I thought you'd be a cold fish."

My jaw tightens in anger.

"So you can run along now."

"I was just a joke to you?"

Her lips curve into a cruel smile. "Have you ever been anything else?"

I blink rapidly. I have to get out of here before I faint.

This was all a prank? He won over my trust, and I gave myself to him thinking he loved me.

I thought he broke my heart all those years ago when he moved on from me, but that's nothing compared with the pain I feel now.

"Get out, Cassie. No one wants you."

My heart's pounding as I turn and walk away. I can't even remember walking down the stairs, but somehow I'm at the base of them and escaping through the crowd in the living room toward the front door.

Once I'm outside, I take in large gulps of fresh air to try and stop myself from crying.

"Cassie. Wait."

I turn to look behind me. Dave runs out the front door of the house.

"What's going on? You're white as a sheet."

Holding up my palms, I make him keep his distance.

"You are the last person I want to talk to right now."

He grabs my arm, and I attempt to pull away but his grip's too strong.

"Stop. I'm not trying to upset you."

"Since when, Dave? Why do you care how I feel? You never have before."

He lets me go. "Because maybe I didn't like you, but I do like Patrick. I spoke to him earlier and apologised for everything I ever did to you because I realise now how lame it all was. And I know he's gonna be pissed if someone upset you."

I shake my head. "I doubt he'll care."

Dave frowns. "What's wrong?"

I close my eyes, tears rolling down my cheeks. "It doesn't matter. I'm going home. Have fun."

He calls out as I walk off but doesn't come after me. As if he really cares. He's been in the thick of it with Vicki and her mean-girl friends for years.

Mum's standing in the foyer when I walk through the door, slamming it behind me.

"Cassie? What's wrong."

I shake my head. "I can't …"

She frowns. "Did something happen at the party? Does your father need to go over there?"

"No. Just please, leave me alone for a bit."

I run up the stairs two at a time, closing the door to my room after I enter it.

As soon as I'm safe, I let out a sob and bite down on my fist.

How could he do it?

I was in that bed with him two weeks ago.

He told me he loved me—he told me it was his first time too. Was any of that true?

In a few days, he'll be gone, and I'm not sure what I'll do when I see him again. Will he even care?

———

I'M NOT sure what time I fell asleep—I think I cried until I passed out from the pounding headache and the wet pillow, but a tap on the door forces me to open my eyes.

"Cassie? Patrick's here to see you," Dad calls.

"I don't care."

The door clicks, and he steps into the room. "Your mother told me something happened. What do I need to do?"

"Tell him to go away." I sniff. My body's so dry I think I cried out every bit of moisture in it, but somehow tears well. "I don't want to see him."

He nods. "Whatever you want, love."

The door closes again, and his heavy footfall disappears into the distance.

The sound of the front door opening floats up to my window.

"I don't know what you did, but she doesn't want to see you." My dad sounds so serious. But I guess he's never had to deal with me being so heartbroken. At least he's not interrogating me to find out why—just swinging in to protect me.

"Cassie," Patrick calls. "I know you're up there. Please, baby, talk to me. I don't know what's going on."

"Doesn't know what's going on," I grumble.

"I've got to go, but I'm not giving up on us," he yells up at my window, and I smack the back of my head against my pillow. "I love you."

It's quiet for a little while before the door opens again, and I turn my head as Mum approaches my bed.

"Cassie?" She sits on the edge and raises her palm to my cheek. "He sounds heartbroken. What happened?"

Tears spill down my cheeks. "He cheated on me."

Confusion crosses Mum's expression before she shakes her head. "No, I can't believe it."

"I saw him. He was in bed with Vicki when I got to the party."

She wraps her arms around me. "Oh, sweetheart. I'm so sorry. He was acting like he didn't know what happened."

"He knows. He looked straight at me and said my name. He'd been drinking, but that's no excuse."

"No. No, it's not."

I breathe in *her*. Mum wears vanilla, and it's the scent that gives me comfort. It always has been, and now is no exception.

"I know it hurts," she whispers. "But one day you'll look back on this and wonder why you worried about it."

I shake my head. "No, I love him, Mum."

She leans back and gazes into my eyes. "I know you did. But he wasn't the right one for you. If he was, he'd never have done this. One day you'll find the right one. I promise."

"I'm such an idiot. He never loved me."

She frowns. "Are you sure about that? He adores you, Cassie. It's in his eyes every time he looks at you."

"It was all some sick prank. He's been with Vicki all along."

Mum shakes her head. "That can't be right."

"That's what she told me last night. And he was right there not saying a word."

"Oh, sweetheart." Her jaw tightens. "If you don't want to see him, we'll keep him out. Okay? They'll be gone in a few days."

"Not soon enough." I sniff.

"I'm so sorry. I thought he was better than that."

"Me too, Mum. Me too."

9

CASSIE

The house is so quiet.

It's been a month since Patrick left, and I'm still feeling so empty.

In a few days, I pack up and move to Auckland for uni. I'm not sure if I can avoid running into him given we're both studying medicine, but maybe by then my heart will have healed enough to talk to him.

"Cassie. We're going to get some stuff for the garden. Did you want to come for a ride?" Dad calls.

Mum and Dad have been trying to get me out of the house. I've made it into the backyard for some sunshine, but I haven't been able to face going anywhere local.

Maybe today I need to get out of this funk. At least I'll be with them and not alone—if we run into Vicki or any of that crowd, they won't say anything if I'm with my parents.

"Okay."

Mum bites her bottom lip. "Patrick called again. I told

him you didn't want to talk to him, but I really think you should."

I roll my eyes. "Fine. Next time he calls, I'll talk to him. Okay?"

"I know you're hurting, but maybe it would give you some closure. If he's still trying to talk to you after all this time, then maybe things aren't as bad as you think they are."

I shrug. "Maybe dumping me in person is part of their prank."

"He sounds miserable."

"Okay. I'll talk to him. Can we go shopping now?"

Mum smiles at me as I walk out the door and toward the car.

The summer sun beats down and I take a moment to breathe in the sweet air and feel the warmth.

Dad's already in the driver's seat. "Let's go."

"Where are we going?" I open the door and climb into the back seat.

"The garden centre. I want to get some seedlings for the new vege patch," Mum says.

"We could go for lunch afterward too. Maybe somewhere down by the beach?" Dad starts the car.

The beach.

Where Patrick made it clear he wanted me. What a joke that was.

I buckle my seatbelt and then slouch in the seat, crossing my arms.

Mum and Dad chat all the way across town, but I stare out of the window. Every day things get a little easier, but after the weeks I spent with Patrick, it's like I've lost a limb.

It's so hard to wrap my head around the cruelty.

I should have spoken to him before he left, but at that point, I couldn't see past the pain. Not just that he didn't love me, but that he went as far as having sex with me just for what? A bet?

I'm usually a fan of Bunnings—there's so much to look at —but one thing blurs into another as we walk down each aisle and Mum and Dad pick out what they need.

It's not until we're on the way to the beach that I relax. It's a good half an hour away from home, but it's enough that I don't usually run into anyone that I went to school with.

We park near the burger place that Patrick usually took me to when we came down here. I say nothing to Mum and Dad because there's no point ruining their afternoon out. Besides, it's good food.

"Do you know what you want?" Dad asks, looking at the menu.

"Just a hamburger and fries," I say.

"And a drink?"

I nod. "If you get the burger and fries deal, it comes with a drink. I just want a coke."

"You got it." He smiles. "I'll get the same."

"Me too," Mum says.

"Why don't you ladies go and find a seat?" Dad's eyes are back on the menu.

Mum and I walk the short distance to a picnic table nearby. She takes a deep breath of sea air.

For the first time since the party, I feel like I can breathe again.

"It's good to see you smiling." Mum grasps my forearm.

"It's nice to be outside."

"I'm so sorry he broke your heart. I really thought he was a good one."

Tears well in my eyes, and she shakes her head.

"You're about to leave home and live your best life."

"I hope so," I whisper.

She pulls me into her arms, and I relax into her embrace.

"I loved him, Mum. I thought he loved me."

"He's an idiot if he doesn't." She presses a kiss in my hair. "And I could have sworn …"

"I just can't wrap my head around it."

"Neither can I. I should have gone over and spoken to Jane before they left. I'm sure she doesn't know what her boy did."

"Hope you're hungry." Dad drops into the other side of the table and smiles. "Those burgers are huge."

I laugh. "They really are."

"We should come down here more often," he says to Mum. "Sun, surf, and good food."

She beams a smile at him—the one she only shares with him. "That sounds like a great idea."

Seeing them just makes my heart ache more. I know we're young, but they have the kind of love I wanted with Patrick.

The one that lasts for life.

After lunch and a walk on the beach, we head home.

I'm not sure how this move and starting uni is going to go when I'm so distracted by my love life, but I hope once classes start, I can put all this behind me.

Although, with Patrick also going to medical school, I don't know how that's going to work—especially if our paths cross.

The only thing I'm grateful for is the knowledge that Vicki isn't going to university. She used to talk about it in class and how sad she was to be apart from Patrick.

But that doesn't really give me any comfort when I remember what she said to me that day.

It comes out of nowhere.

Glass shatters to the right of me.

I go flying sideways—as much as the seatbelt will allow—my head hitting the window with a heavy thud.

Pain rips through my body right before my vision goes black.

10

CASSIE

"Does she know?"

Know what? My head's swimming, but at least my ears aren't ringing anymore.

"Not yet. When she came in, she was in and out of consciousness, and we had to sedate her to reset the bones."

"Poor thing. Her grandmother's on the way?"

"Yes. Shouldn't be too much longer. She was getting in the car as we spoke."

"Good. She shouldn't be alone."

Alone?

Where are my parents?

What happened?

Where am I?

My eyelids won't open, but that doesn't matter as the heaviness in my head grows and I surrender to it.

When they do open, it's to bright lights.

Beep, beep, beep.

Warmth encloses my hand, and I turn my head.

I haven't seen my grandmother for the past few years—she and Dad had a big falling out. But she's the only grandparent I have left and she's by my bedside.

"Gran?" I croak.

"Do you want some water, sweetheart?"

I nod. I try to sit up, but I'm too weak and my legs—my legs are in traction?

She holds a cup of water to my mouth and I open up as she tips it slightly. The cool water wets my dry mouth, and I sigh with relief.

"Thank you," I say.

She puts down the cup and takes a seat beside me again.

"What happened?"

Gran gives me a sad smile. "You were in an accident."

I nod. "I remember that much."

"I'll let the nurse know you're awake. We need to talk about what's happening."

My eyes are still heavy, and I can't argue. I don't have it in me.

There's noise around me as Gran talks to someone, and I close my eyes again.

Gran slips her hand into mine, and I turn my head to look at her.

She scans my expression, and her eyes grow sad.

"Cassie? I'm Doctor Ludlow." A middle-aged man with kind eyes approaches the bed.

I squint. "I'm sorry. The light ..."

His eyes widen and he nods. "You're in a single room, we can turn those off. There's a lamp above your head."

"Please."

People move around me to make the adjustments and the light dims.

"What do you remember, Cassie?" the doctor asks.

"There was an accident. I don't know what happened. I just remember glass breaking and the force of it, and that was it."

He nods slowly. "I'm very sorry to be the one to tell you this, but your parents didn't make it."

"What?" My heart cracks in two.

"We discussed when to tell you, and your grandmother thought we should be up front with it. I'm so sorry, Cassie."

"She's right. I needed to know, but … oh my God."

Gran gives my hand a squeeze, and I burst into tears.

She leans over and holds me as best she can. How can they both be gone?

"I'll give you a moment."

He steps out, and she kisses my temple.

"I'm so sorry, sweetheart. I wish things had turned out differently. But I'm here for you and I'm not going anywhere."

"What am I going to do without them?"

She strokes my hair. "We take this one day at a time."

We sit together like that for I'm not really sure how long until I give her arm a squeeze. "I need to know what's happening to me."

"I'll go and get the doctor."

She stands and watches me for a moment. "We'll get thought this, Cassie. We'll do it together."

"Thank you for being here," I whisper.

"How could I be anywhere else?"

She turns and walks to the door, and there's a murmured

conversation before she comes back in—the doctor not far behind.

He gives me a sad smile.

"So, let's talk about your injuries. You have two broken legs and two fractures in your spine. We ran some tests—standard procedure before imaging." He glances at my grandmother again. "We'll have to do things a little differently because of your pregnancy. But each surgery is a risk. We'll need to pin both legs and stabilise the bigger fracture in your spine."

"Pregnancy?" I feel like I'm in an alternate reality.

"You didn't know? It's early—we'd need to perform an ultrasound to get the exact date."

I nod. "Can we do that?"

"We'll get a portable ultrasound machine in here."

"Please."

Gran holds my hand tightly. I'm so numb, and it's not just because of my injuries. I've felt like I've been drowning ever since the night I caught Patrick with Vicki, and now I'm underwater and never coming back up.

"Did you suspect?" Gran asks.

I shake my head. "I've been stressed. That plays havoc with my periods."

She nods. "Who's the father?"

Closing my eyes, I let out a sigh. "That's a whole other story to tell you. Can we just get through this first?"

"Of course, sweetheart. We have plenty of time. They tell me that they don't know how long you'll be in here, but afterward, I'll take you home to Hamilton to recuperate."

I force a small smile. When I was a kid, I loved going to Gran's place. She has a cottage that's cosy and comforting.

"What will happen to our house?"

She rubs my arm with her free hand. "Let's worry about that later. One day at a time, Cassie. That's all we can do right now. I'll stay there while you're in here, but I would feel better taking you home."

"I'd like that," I whisper.

———

IT'S A BLOB.

At least that's what it looks like, but apparently that's my baby—mine and Patrick's.

I don't know what to do. If my life was easier, or if Patrick was still here and we were together, I wouldn't have a decision to make.

"It's early." The doctor points at the screen. "The next few weeks in particular will be hard as you recover. If you want to proceed with the pregnancy, then pain relief becomes more difficult. And you have surgery ahead as we'll need to put surgical pins in both your legs and address your spinal fractures."

"What do you think I should do?"

"I can't help you make that decision. What I can do is tell you the risks involved, and it will be a harder road as far as pain goes. There's no reason for this pregnancy not to work out, but it is higher risk as a result." He smiles. "The things you do have on your side are the fact that you're young and healthy otherwise. It really is up to you, Cassie. The medical team here will support you whatever your decision."

"So will I," Gran says, giving my hand a squeeze.

"I want to keep it. The only other family I have is Gran. I need … I need something to look forward to."

"Then that's what you'll do." Gran nods.

Maybe it should be a hard decision, but really, it's the easiest decision in the world. The baby is my link to my past and no matter how much things hurt, I'll always have a little piece of Patrick with me.

Of course, I have to tell him, but right now I have no way of contacting him. I don't know his parents' new number, and I have no idea where my mobile phone is. His number is programmed into it, so I don't even know what that is.

For now, I'll concentrate on getting through the next few weeks. I don't even know if he'll take it well, given the way things ended with him.

Is he with Vicki now?

Everything is such a mess.

11

CASSIE

I t took three surgeries in the end. The initial one, where they put the pins in to realign my legs, and when one of my legs didn't heal right, they had to re-break it and redo the surgery.

Thankfully, that worked.

There was also an operation for one of my spinal fractures where a plate and screws were put in place.

On top of that, there was a discussion about skin grafts as there'd been a fire in the car. It was put out quickly but because it took so long to extract me, I had burns on my back along with the scarring from the surgery.

But I made the choice not to do that—to at least delay it until after my baby was born.

Seven months after the accident, weighing in at seven pound, four ounces, Sophie Jane Warren was born.

I'm not even sure why I gave her Patrick's mother's name

as a middle name. Maybe it was to form a connection with a family she might never know.

But it felt like the right thing to do along with my mother's middle name—Sophie.

With everything I've been through, the hormones after childbirth hit hard.

One minute I want to go to Patrick and throw it all in his face. The next, I want to bury my head under the covers and pretend he doesn't exist.

But he does, and I see him in my daughter's face.

Babies' eyes might change colour, but Sophie's are a piercing blue just like his and there's a part of me that hopes they stay the same.

She's so beautiful.

Whatever happens in her life, she'll always have me.

I'm anxious all over again about tracking down Patrick and telling him. He needs to at least know she exists. She's already two months old.

Nerves eat at me as I place her in her capsule and make my way out to my car.

"It's good to see you out and about," Gran calls from the doorway.

"I'm going to Auckland. I have to find him."

She walks toward the car and waits as I clip Sophie in and close the door.

"Are you sure about this?"

I shrug. "I have no idea, but it's eating me up."

"Maybe you should wait until things have settled down."

I know she means well, but I need to do this.

Sophie needs her father—although, what do I do if he rejects her?

Tears well in my eyes. "Maybe, but I want to try."

She takes my hand in hers. "Then I hope things work out the way you need them to. I'll be here when you come back."

I swallow hard. No matter what happens, Gran has my back. She's all the family I have left.

Closing my eyes, I let her pull me into her arms.

It's probably not a good idea to go when I'm so up and down, but I think Gran understands I have to get this out of my system. Even some time away from the house would be good.

"Drive safe," she whispers.

I nod. There's no way I'll take any risks with Sophie in the car. I struggle with the fact that my parents will never know their granddaughter, and she's the most precious person in my life along with Gran.

She always has to come first.

And whether she has her father in her life or not, I'll always be there for her.

I climb into the driver's seat and take a deep breath before starting the car.

"Let's go for a drive, baby girl."

It's not a long drive—about an hour and a half with a break in the middle to feed Sophie, but Auckland always intimidates me.

Hamilton is bigger and busier than Hastings is, but Auckland is on a whole other level.

We used to come up here on family trips to go to the zoo and do other sightseeing, and driving here myself is a new adventure.

I have no real idea where I'm going.

Maybe this is insane.

I lost my mobile phone in the car accident, and Gran replaced it for me. I didn't complain about the change in number—she did it while I was in hospital so she could call me when she wasn't there. But I've also lost all my contacts, and I didn't memorise any of the numbers.

Patrick's parents aren't in the white pages—I tried looking them up. And I don't know where they moved to.

The only way this is going to work is if I go to the university and pray for the best.

Once I'm off the motorway, I slow and make my way closer to the medical school.

I shouldn't have come.

This was stupid.

It's too soon.

I need to be in a better place mentally for this.

Pulling in under a tree, I take a deep breath.

Gran knew—she knew this was a mistake. But she also loves me enough to let me make them. If she'd tried to stop me, I'm not sure it would have worked. I'd probably have dug my heels in.

I lean back on the headrest and close my eyes, getting my breathing under control.

It's all too raw.

Patrick is one thing too. What about his parents? Are they going to hate me for having a baby and not telling them?

I can't do this.

I open my eyes.

Students flood out into the streets—they must have just been released from lectures.

My heart pangs—this is what I've been waiting for.

He's there.

It's probably too far for him to work out that it's me, but Patrick walks onto the footpath and comes to a stop.

From near my car, a woman calls out his name and runs down the street toward him.

He catches her before kissing her. It's not a passionate kiss, but not a peck.

Is that his girlfriend?

She's tall, slim, and blonde—reminiscent of Vicki.

My heart cracks open a little wider.

For a moment, I watch them. She's animated, waving her arms around as she speaks. He takes a step back, but studies her closely—enough it's clear he's engaged in whatever she's saying.

She grabs hold of his hand and runs her own up his arm.

There's intimacy there.

He's moved on.

Of course he has—he moved on the night of the party.

Sophie stirs, and I glance in the rear-view mirror. She's what's important. Will he even want her? I shouldn't have come so soon after giving birth.

I'm an emotional mess.

I can't do this today.

After starting the car, I reverse into the street and take one more look in Patrick's direction.

The distance between us is too far to make out his expression, but a shiver runs through me as it seems like our gazes lock.

I draw in a deep breath and drive away before I can change my mind—again.

This will have to wait for another day. I'm not sure I'm in

any kind of emotional state to introduce him *and* his girl-friend to our daughter.

The farther I get from the university, the more I relax.

And then we're back on the motorway, making our way home to Hamilton where Gran and safety are.

"I THOUGHT you'd be gone longer than this," she says as I walk in the door, baby capsule in hand.

"I couldn't do it. I think he's moved on."

Dropping onto the couch, I place Sophie's car seat on the floor before unbuckling her and lifting her out. She smells of baby powder and zinc. It's comforting and familiar.

"You saw him?"

"From a distance. He was with his girlfriend. At least, I assume she's his girlfriend from the way they kissed each other."

She frowns. "I'm so sorry, love."

"I had to get out of there. What was I supposed to say in front of her?"

Gran sits beside me and slips an arm around my waist. "You'll tell him in good time."

I nod. "He needs to know. Just not today."

She gives me a kiss on the cheek. "Whatever you need."

12

PATRICK

Melissa throws herself at me, and I have no option but to catch her.

She plants a kiss on my lips, and I gently shake her off.

I stand back as she tells me about her day. She's studying medicine too, and I made the mistake of going out with her a couple of times before telling her we can't be anything more than friends.

I'm still too raw over what happened last summer.

I tried to speak to Cassie, but something happened at that party that made her blank me. She blocked me on her mobile, and eventually calling the house stopped working, like the line had been disconnected or something.

So I went back after the first semester, and no one was home—the only person I saw was Dave Pratt, but he didn't know anything. I couldn't afford to stick around, so I headed back to Auckland a couple of days later.

She didn't want anything more to do with me.

I'm not really listening to Melissa, and I run my gaze down the road.

Is that Cassie's car?

No. I must be imagining things.

Melissa runs her hand up my arm, and I shoot a glare at her.

Turning back, I try and focus on the car—I'm sure I'd recognise Cassie's car anywhere. I thought for sure I'd be able to catch up with her when she started university, but she never did.

I start to walk toward it, but it backs into the street.

My heart sinks and I pick up my pace until I break into a run, but it's gone and I reach where it was parked and look in the direction it went.

Could it have been her?

"Patrick." Melissa runs after me. "What's going on?"

"Nothing." I run my fingers through my hair. "I'm going home."

"Don't you want to go and get a drink?"

I turn toward her. She's objectively gorgeous with long blonde hair and legs that go on for days. But I'm just not interested in her that way.

She's made it more than clear that she is.

"I'm sorry if I ever made you think there could be anything between us."

"Are you kidding me?"

That flash of anger reminds me so much of Vicki. I don't want to go back to that either. "No, I'm not. And I never pretended to be more interested than I was. We went out a couple of times and that was it."

Her lower lip wobbles.

But my mind's in such a mess that I can't even worry about her being upset.

"Anyway, I've got to go." I walk away before she says anything else and make my way to the bus stop.

It's a short ride home.

The kitchen is quiet—Dad's not home yet, and Mum sits on the couch watching afternoon TV.

She frowns when I walk in and dump my bag on a chair.

"Are you okay?"

"Why?"

"You look … agitated."

I sit next to her on the couch. "I thought I saw Cassie's car today."

Mum rolls her eyes. "If she hasn't been here this past year, why would she suddenly turn up?"

"I don't know. Maybe she delayed coming here a year?"

She sighs. "Patrick. We've been through this. For whatever reason, she decided to cut you out of her life. It was awful and cruel and hurt you deeply. I don't want you rehashing this and going back to where you were at the start of the year."

I meet her gaze. She's right. I was a mess when we arrived here. All I wanted was to understand what had happened, and no one would give me any answers.

My beautiful girl dumped me.

Maybe today was wishful thinking.

Will I ever see her again?

13

CASSIE

Five years later

"Sophie Warren, you'd better hustle."

My daughter drags her feet as she walks from the hallway to the dining table. She's so adorable in her school uniform—I'll never get over her being old enough to go to school.

"Eat up, sweetheart. We've got to get going soon."

"Why?" She sits and picks up a slice of toast.

"We've got a builder coming today to start the renovations Mr Smedley's organised."

She pauses mid-bite. "Like Bob?"

I laugh. "Yes, just like Bob the Builder. Now finish your breakfast and brush your teeth so we can get out of here."

Sophie's the best thing that ever happened to me.

It's been a tough few years but we have our routine now, and she's such a good kid.

Once she's ready for school, I drive the short distance to drop her off. With me working full time, Sophie's in before and after school care. The day is longer, but we make up for it over the weekends by lazing around.

I live for those times.

After I've dropped her off, I head to work.

At twenty-four, I thought I'd be finishing medical school and moving onto clinical training. Instead, I started work at nineteen at a local casual clothing store and was promoted at the beginning of the year to store manager.

The owner and I just clicked. He knew Gran, and when he hired me, I worked my arse off to prove myself as I had my daughter to provide for.

He treats me like I'm his long, lost daughter—when Gran died two years ago, I grew even closer with him and his wife.

I think he was looking for an excuse to retire early and grabbed it with both hands as I showed an interest in all aspects of running the store. He still takes care of things like the budgets and accounts, but I manage the day to day operations.

I'm lucky my co-workers like me and none of them were interested in moving up in the business.

I get there on time to open up and let the staff of five in.

And then I go about my day.

I'm nervous about the renovations. I'll have to juggle the store still being open while things are changed around—and I know nothing about the changes.

Mr Smedley's not quite yet ready to let go of that.

"Cassie, could I get some help putting this stock out?"

Colleen, one of the older ladies who's worked here forever, asks.

"Sure thing."

They get busy. We sell both men's and women's clothing, and although I'm now ordering stock, the lingering boss still sticks his nose in sometimes and more stock arrives than we can handle.

But we have learned to take things in our stride.

I get busy folding T-shirts, and between us, we've nearly got the display done when Mr Smedley walks in.

The man beside him does a double take at me, and I study him curiously.

"Cassie. I'd like you to meet Mark Burrows." Mr Smedley beams. "This is my store manager, Cassie. She's your point of contact for any questions you have about … well … anything." He laughs.

Mark smiles and it lights up his whole face. He's clearly older than me—I'm going to guess maybe thirty-fiveish, and when I shake his offered hand, it's rough as if battered by years of hard work.

"Mr Smedley's told me nothing about what's happening, so I was hoping you could fill me in." I grin.

I love my boss—most of the time.

He's been organising this outside of hours, and I'm hoping it encompasses all the things we've discussed that need updating.

"Let's do a walk through and we'll talk," Mr Smedley says. "Mark and I have been going over about how to do things with minimal disruption. How that works in practice, well, I guess we'll find out."

I smile. This building has barely been updated in forty years, but it's solid and doesn't need much. The layout leaves a lot to be desired. I've been wanting to revamp the dated changing rooms since I started here, which is the big one on the list.

It doesn't take long, and the changes all make sense. Restructuring the changing rooms so we have more cubicles as the current ones are huge. And enclosing the office space at the back as it's currently quite open with a cash register in case the others are busy.

I wanted that change.

We never use that register and closing the whole area off makes it more secure.

Mr Smedley apparently agreed.

"I'll leave you in Cassie's capable hands," Mr Smedley says.

"That sounds good to me." Mark never drops eye contact. It doesn't make me uncomfortable—I'm no expert, but I think he's interested. And he's such a good-looking man, I don't mind.

When he's gone, Mark turns to me. "I'll get set up today if that works for you. I'd like to start with the changing rooms as that's probably the biggest change and we can do one side at a time. Not that we'll get the reno started today, but we need to put up signage and block off the actual construction."

I nod. "That'd be good."

Mark smiles. "Maybe you could work with me to decide where it goes?"

His dark eyes dance, and for the first time since Patrick, my heart does little pitter-patters. This guy is gorgeous—

there's no way he'd be interested in a woman with the baggage I have.

This is stupid.

I'm not going to be a sucker for a man again.

"Sure thing. Let's get this out of the way."

"Once it's done, we'll start moving gear in here so we can get started in the morning if that works."

"Sounds fine."

We move quickly, and before too long his guys set up a barrier to stop people from entering the work space. With the signage up, I'm confident that they can work in peace—as much as working in an open store will allow.

It's not going to be fun, but it's also not going to take too long.

They start shifting in gear, and I move on to other things around the store.

Before I know it, it's nearly time to close.

One by one, the cash registers are totalled for the day and closed. Once the takings are all in the safe and the staff have gone, I turn off the lights and make my way to the door.

Maybe tonight I'll grab some takeaways on the way home. We don't have them often, but it's been a long and fruitful day.

I lock the front door and take a step in the direction of my car.

"Cassie."

I turn. Mark walks toward me, a cautious smile on his face.

"Is there something else you need? I've got to go and pick up my daughter, but I can spare a few minutes if I need to unlock."

He shakes his head. "No. Nothing inside the store, anyway."

Butterflies rise in my stomach. "So, how can I help you?"

His cheeks redden and he looks at his feet a moment before meeting my gaze again. "I was hoping you'd go out with me some time."

I bite my bottom lip. This is unexpected. For the past few years, I've been head down working to support myself and Sophie. When Gran passed, she left me the house, so I'm lucky enough not to have to worry about rent, but doing this alone is hard.

I've thought about dating, but it all just seemed too difficult to go out and meet new people.

"I'd like that."

His eyes light up. "Really? That's great. Maybe we could go for coffee tomorrow?"

I nod. "That sounds good."

He grins. "See you tomorrow, Cassie Warren."

"See you tomorrow."

I turn to unlock the car, pausing before I get in. He has a bounce in his step as he walks away, and it makes me feel all giddy.

It's so far from the high school days of not being sure if I was being pranked—we're adults and he likes me. I like the look of him.

He didn't even flinch at the mention of my daughter.

If I'm going to be with anyone else, they need to know up front that she's my whole life.

Nothing and no one is more important than her.

14

CASSIE

I'm so busy first thing that I almost forget about agreeing to go for coffee with Mark.

He doesn't.

He stalks toward me midmorning, and my heart flutters.

"Hi," he says.

"Hi."

"I didn't see you earlier."

"Oh, I've been busy out back. We're getting close to doing our stocktake, and there's a ton of things to organise."

He grins. "Do you think we could go for coffee? To discuss the store changes."

"The store changes?" I can't help but smile. For the first time in my life, I'm a hundred per cent sure someone's flirting with me.

"Of course." He grins back.

"I guess I'll have to." I place my hand on my chest. "If it's work related."

Mark chuckles. "Maybe not completely work related."

"Now the truth comes out."

"Please?" His dark eyes dance with mischief, and I'm sucked in even further.

"I'd like that very much."

"How about lunch today?"

I hold up my palms. "Whoa, from coffee to lunch? That's way too fast."

His face falls.

"I'm kidding, Mark. I'd love to have lunch with you."

His eyes twinkle and his lips spread into a smile again. "Around midday?"

I nod. "Sounds good. We could go to the cafe across the road."

"See you then."

The rest of morning is busy. It can be chaotic enough without workmen, but Mark's team does a good job of keeping out of the way and while the noise can get a bit loud, it's all workable.

At midday, he appears in the door of my office, folding his arms and leaning against the doorframe.

With his sleeves rolled up, he's got that forearm porn going on, and my heart gives a little flutter in response.

I like this—it's been so long since I felt anything.

In a single day, Mark's made me feel alive again.

"Ready to eat?"

"Famished." I pick up my bag and flick my hair over my shoulder. My heart thuds as I walk toward him, and he flashes me a bright smile.

"Good. I hear they do good meals over there."

"I love their BLT."

His brows knit. "Oooh that sounds good."

"I'd kill a coffee too."

Mark tilts his head toward the front of the store. "Come on, then."

We make our way out of the store together. I hold my head up. Gossip will surround me, but I don't care. I deserve this.

I deserve some happiness.

Even if one lunch is all it is, for a little while I can be selfish and think of myself.

———

"So, tell me about you."

I blush. "I don't know what to tell you. I'm a single mother of a five-year-old who manages the store for Mr Smedley."

He chuckles. "I wasn't sure if I should ask you out after you said something about picking up your daughter. Didn't want to stand on any toes."

I hold up my palms. "Oh, there are no toes to stand on."

"I find that hard to believe."

I can't help it, my smile's so wide my face aches.

"Well, it's true. I thought you'd run a mile when I mentioned my daughter."

He shrugs. "She's part of your package. And it's a very attractive package from what I can see."

Laughing, I take a sip of my coffee. "Stop it."

"No. I like making you smile."

"Are you always such an outrageous flirt?"

Mark shoots me a wink. "Only with the pretty clients."

I bark out another laugh. "You're terrible."

"I'm pretty nice, actually. And I really want to see you again."

I bite my bottom lip. I was sure he was just flirting, but this just got serious. I've not thought about dating in, well, forever.

"I'll need to think about it."

His brows knit. "I hope I didn't come on too strong."

I shake my head. "No, it's just … I haven't dated anyone since before my daughter was born. The last person I was seeing was her father. And he isn't in the picture. But she's all I have now, and I have to think about her first."

Mark nods. "I understand. And I want you to know that I get it. I was twenty when my parents died, and my little sister was ten. I took over raising her after that, and I would do anything for that girl. Although, she's not really a girl anymore."

I grasp his forearm. "I'm so sorry for your loss."

"It's not easy. I get that. But maybe you're owed a little happiness."

"You think you can give me that?"

His eyes twinkle. "I know I can. I'm not looking for a one-night stand or anything shady. I'd really like to spend time with you."

I draw in a deep breath. "I think I'd like that too. Give me some time?"

He gazes at me as if he'll never see me again. "Take all the time in the world. I'll be waiting."

———

HIS WORDS PLAY on my mind the rest of the day.

As I pull into the school car park, I'm still thinking about what he said.

It feels like he can really relate to what I've been through with his own experiences.

And he's such a nice guy.

I'm not sure what to do.

"Mummy." Sophie runs at me as if she hasn't seen me in forever. It's the best part of the after-school-care pick-up.

I open my arms, and she throws herself into them. God, how I love this kid.

"Have you had a good day?"

She nods. "I read some words for Mrs Crawford today."

"Did you?" She's a smart cookie. I think between me and Patrick, she was always going to be. I'm so proud of her.

"And I wrote my name. She told me it was perfect."

"It is. You are." I tap her on the nose, and she giggles. "How about we get home and get some dinner?"

"Can we have butter chicken?"

I roll my eyes. "You'll turn into a chicken if we have it any more often."

She lets go of me, flaps her arms, and squawks.

"Okay, okay. Butter chicken it is. Let's go home. I'm tired."

After dinner, she has her bath and gets into her pyjamas. I'm not sure who's more sleepy—me or her.

Busy days always wear me out.

She climbs onto the couch with me. This is the favourite part of my day.

"Sophie? What would you say if I started seeing someone?"

She rolls her eyes. "You see me."

I laugh. "No, a man. Like dating."

"What's dating?"

I blow out a breath. This is harder than I thought, and not in the way I thought.

"It's when two people like each other and want to spend time together."

"And kiss?"

I smile. "Maybe."

"I think you should have some kisses, Mummy."

Laughing, I peck her temple. "I like your kisses."

She snuggles into my side, and I close my eyes. I think so often of telling Patrick about her, but the longer I take, the harder it gets. After that ill-fated trip to Auckland, I struggled with depression and was so grateful I had Gran.

By the time I was okay again, I had to have one of my legs re-broken and re-pinned as it hadn't healed correctly the first time. Then there was a further surgery with the skin graft where I'd been burned on my spine.

And then Gran died.

Since then, I've been running on fumes. Just meeting someone who sparked my interest and who is interested in me is something I'm going to hang onto for a long time.

No matter how things work out.

———

MARK'S up a ladder when I approach the following morning.

He glances down at me as I walk toward him.

"Oh, hey, love. You okay?"

I smile at the term of endearment and nod. "Fine. How's it going?"

He beams. "We're making good progress. This lot should be done by the end of the week and then we can move over to the other side. Then we'll look at those office changes."

"Great." I fidget, and he looks at me again before stepping down the rungs of the ladder one by one.

When we're level, he grabs hold of my hands until they stop trembling.

"That's better. What's going on?"

"Yes. I want to say yes."

"Yes?"

"To going out with you. It's okay with Sophie. So, I want to say yes."

His face lights up like a Christmas tree. "Really?"

I nod. "Yes."

"Do you have any idea how much I want to kiss you right now, Cassie Warren?"

I laugh. "My daughter did say I should have some kisses."

"When can we make that happen?" He tilts his head. "The date, I mean. Not the kisses. Although, I can make that happen too."

My cheeks flush. "The weekend? My neighbour will babysit."

"Saturday night. We'll go out for dinner if that works for you."

"I'd like that."

As I walk away, there's an extra skip to my step. Maybe it's time I moved on with my life.

Maybe Mark's just what I need.

15

CASSIE

For our first date, we arrange to meet at the restaurant.

I'm not sure about introducing Sophie to anyone too quickly, and Mark understands that.

In fact, he's incredibly understanding about everything.

Mrs McIntyre is only too happy to come over to stay with Sophie, and I'm so grateful to her. She's lived next to Gran's house for years, and the two of them were good friends.

So, when Gran died and I needed help, she would turn up every time.

Sophie kisses me goodbye—the good part about Mrs McIntyre being a part of our lives for so long is that Sophie doesn't get upset when I leave. She's been through that phase, and I hated every second of being apart from her.

I still don't like it much, but I do what I have to so we have food on the table.

Tonight is the first time I've put myself first in a long time.

"Have a good night, Cassie. Just remember I'm happy to sleep over if you want to stay out." Mrs McIntyre winks at me. She's not exactly subtle about pushing me to move on.

It's not a long drive across town, but it gives me time to think. I like Mark. I think he'll be good for us. Over the past week, while he's been working in the store, he's flirted with me but he hasn't pushed. He's kind and gentle, but I've also heard him being firm with his workers and he doesn't take any kind of shit.

I'm not about to rush into anything with him, but I'm also going to go with the flow.

I have to keep reminding myself that I'm a grown woman and not that insecure eighteen-year-old I was the first time around. The thought of being with an older man intrigues me too.

I'll never forget the one and only time I was with Patrick, and how neither of really knew what we were doing but we found pleasure together.

What would it be like with Mark?

I pull up to the restaurant and park outside.

Mark waits at the door, and I take in the sight of him dressed in a smart shirt and dress pants—a far cry from the T-shirt and jeans he wears at work.

His face lights up as I approach, and he reaches for my hand when I draw level with him.

Lacing his fingers in mine, he smiles. "I'm glad you made it."

"I wasn't about to stand you up."

His rough skin feels good against mine as he gives my hand a squeeze and leads me into the restaurant.

"Table for Burrows," he tells the maître d'.

"This way, sir."

I'm not sure I've ever been somewhere this nice. Is this really his kind of thing or is he out to impress? I'd much rather have a burger and fries somewhere than go somewhere fancy. Tonight I'll enjoy being pampered. Next time, I'll …

Next time?

I'm already thinking about our next date.

My cheeks flush as we take our seats, and Mark looks at me curiously.

"What were you just thinking about?" he asks.

"Just how nice this place is."

He grins. "I wanted to take you somewhere fancy. It's not really my kind of thing."

"So why are we here?" I cross my arms.

He chuckles. "To make a good impression. And I've always wanted to try it. My sister's been here a few times and she said the food is really good."

I pick up the menu from the table and raise my eyebrows. "It had better be at these prices."

"So what were you *really* thinking about?"

I narrow my eyes. "How do you do that?"

"Do what?"

"Know that that wasn't what I was thinking."

He leans back in his chair. "Your cheeks weren't red because you were thinking about the restaurant. I hope you were thinking about me."

I burst out laughing. "Actually, I thought next time we'll

just go and get a burger or something because this isn't my kind of place. But I'm happy to be here with you."

"So you want there to be a next time?"

I shrug. "Let's see how tonight goes."

Dinner is amazing. The food is great, and the company even better.

Mark makes me laugh, and it feels like forever since I've just enjoyed another person's company.

He's a smart man who's run his own business for years, and I admire the fact that he raised his sister.

His flirting is outrageous, and I love every minute of it. It's so good to know exactly where I stand, and I don't have any doubts about ulterior motives.

I've never been so relaxed.

Afterward, he insists on paying the bill and walks me to my car.

We slow as we approach it, and he reaches for my hand.

"I really want to kiss you."

"Then maybe you should," I whisper.

He cups my cheek and leans in. His lips press firmly on mine, his tongue probing for entry.

It's now or never.

I open, and his tongue sweeps across mine. His lips are so soft and warm, and I'm left in no doubt as to how he's feeling.

"Oh, there's definitely going to be a next time." He pecks me on the lips. "Drive safe. See you on Monday."

My heart's in my throat as I drive home.

Could Mark Burrows be my happy ending?

16

CASSIE

By the time Mark's birthday rolls around, we've been on several dates.

Things with him are different—I'm in love again, but it feels more grown up.

I kiss Sophie's head. "Be good."

"She's always good for me," Mrs McIntyre says.

She's staying the night this time. I don't have any definitive plans to stay with Mark, but it made sense to me to cover my bases.

I'm nervous but I know he wants me, and I want him.

He has yet to meet Sophie, but the idea that I'm a single mother doesn't scare him. He's made it very clear that he's interested, and I want to explore an adult relationship with him—if he's up for that.

"Love you, Mum." Sophie hugs me tight. "You look pretty."

"Thank you, my love."

"Have a good night, Cassie," Mrs McIntyre says.

I wave before I make my way out to the car and drive to Mark's place.

The party's in full swing when I get there.

Music beats—a song I don't know—but all I can hear is the bass line at first. Mark's clearly popular and his house is full of people.

I don't know anyone.

Maybe this wasn't such a good idea.

It's been a long time since I've been around so many people—the last party I went to was Patrick's.

As I scan the crowd, I meet the gaze of a tall, dark-haired man not far from me.

His lips curl into a smile and he covers the short distance between us quickly.

"Hey," he says.

My skin crawls as he casts his sleazy gaze over me. "I don't know you."

"No. No, you don't. But we could change that."

I shake my head. "I don't think so. I'm here for Mark."

He snorts. "Half the women at this party are here for Mark."

My heart sinks.

"He's a bit of a man whore, you know? Gets around."

For a moment, I'm thrown, but I straighten myself out and stare him down. "Are you supposed to be one of his friends?"

He grins. "We've known each other for years."

"So why are you trashing him?"

His mouth falls open, but a squeal to my left gets my attention.

"You must be Cassie."

A blonde bombshell with curls in her hair and smelling of flowers descends on me, wrapping an arm around my shoulders and giving me a side hug.

"I am."

"Mark's been so nervous waiting for you to get here. Let me take you to him."

I turn, meeting her brown-eyed gaze. "That would be great."

"Cassie, is it?" the creepy guy says.

The blonde's nostril's flare. "Come on."

She pulls me away.

"Thank you for that."

I really hope she's not one of Mark's women. She's a similar age to me, I think, but she's flawless. I feel dumpy in comparison.

"What did Ian say to you?"

I roll my eyes. "He was hitting on me, and trashing Mark in the process."

She narrows her eyes. "He was what?"

"I'm sorry. Is he your boyfriend?"

She laughs and shakes her head. "No, he's an old friend of Mark's, but he's just creepy. I don't know why Mark still lets him hang around."

I swallow hard. She's clearly close to Mark. Why am I here?

"I've told him before he's a sleaze, but they've known each other since primary school, so they've been friends forever. He doesn't do crap like that to me because he knows Mark would punch him." She snorts. "Anyway, Mark's just over here."

She leads me to a corner of the room where Mark is, a beer in hand. Two men stand with him and they're all laughing about something when I catch his eye.

"Cassie. I'm so glad you made it." He makes a beeline for me and pecks me on the cheek. "I see you've met Lauren."

Her eyes widen and she splays a palm on her chest. "I'm so sorry I didn't introduce myself. I'm Mark's younger and much better-looking sibling."

"Hey," Mark says sounding wounded, but with a smile.

I laugh. "It's good to meet you."

"I found Cassie being cornered by Ian. I don't know why you don't tell him to bugger off."

Mark rolls his eyes. "He's an old friend, Lauren. You know that."

"Yeah? Would you have been happy if he'd got off with the one woman you actually want here?"

He gulps. "No. But I don't think he'd do that."

She shifts her gaze back to me. "Make that better looking and *smarter* sibling."

I can't help but bark out another laugh and grin at her. "I like you."

"Thanks." She cuffs her brother's ear. "I love this dipshit, but he's trying at times. You'll soon find out."

"Ouch." Mark chuckles and rubs the side of his head. "Okay. I get the message."

"I'm going to get another drink. It's good to finally meet you, Cassie." She turns on her heel and walks off.

I take a deep breath and face Mark.

"Was he really that bad?"

I shrug. "I didn't like the way he was looking at me."

He frowns. "What about the way *I* look at you?"

My heart's in my throat. I like Mark—really like him. I need to be bold and tell him that, not hide behind my awkwardness. "I like the way *you* look at me."

His lips curl into a smile. "I'll talk to Ian. Want to get out of here?"

"Isn't this your birthday party?"

His smile grows. "It is, but no one's allowed upstairs. We could go up to my room."

I take a step closer. "What's in your room, Mr Burrows?"

"A chance for some peace and quiet so we can talk?" His eyes twinkle, and it's clear he's thinking about more than talking.

But I'm ready.

I'm ready to find my happiness.

"Lead the way."

He curls his fingers around mine. I follow as he makes his way through the party and toward the stairs. Ian stands by the base of them and scowls when he sees us.

"Ian. This is my lady, Cassie."

He nods. "We met."

"Yeah, so don't hit on her."

His gaze snaps to me, but Mark uses his free hand to grab his arm. "If I hear about you making anyone else uncomfortable, we can't be friends."

"Oh come on. She's just—"

"I mean it. She's not *just* anything."

My heart swells. Over the past few weeks, this attraction has been bubbling away and tonight might just be the night we're together as a couple.

I'd like that.

"She's my girl." Mark wraps an arm around me. This is

what I like about him—this is what I need. He makes me feel safe.

"Noted." Ian takes a slug of his beer.

"Let's go up to my room and get away from everyone."

I blow out a long breath as we mount the stairs, the noise of the party fading when we reach his room and close the door behind us.

His room is so *him*.

The walls are a mix of wood and dark tones—the large bed at one end features a beautifully carved headboard.

It's all very manly and probably a bit over the top, but I love it.

"You act like you don't want a party."

He chuckles. "I don't. It was Lauren's idea. She sometimes likes to party a little too much, but I don't mind indulging her when she's at home and I know she's safe."

"You live together? I never thought to ask."

Mark nods. "It's a long story. But I'd rather she be under this roof than anywhere else."

"I can understand that."

He takes a step toward me. "I'd love it if you stayed with me tonight. We'll leave the rest of them shut out and stay in here."

My heart races. "I'd love to."

"You've got a babysitter for the night?"

My cheeks flush with heat. "My neighbour's staying over."

He raises his hand to cup my neck. "I like a woman who plans ahead."

I press my palms to his chest. "I like you."

His eyes flash with excitement. "Maybe I'll just show you how much I want to be with you because I like you too."

"I won't say no."

And then he kisses me, and for the first time in years I can see my future.

I'm so crazy about Mark Burrows.

17

CASSIE

Eight years later

"I'm so sorry."

I gaze at the doctor. Mark and I decided to try for a baby two years ago. With nothing happening, we went through what seemed like a million tests to see what the problem was, and we just got the news.

We've stumbled at the first hurdle.

Mark's sperm count is low—very low.

Mark squeezes my knee. "At least we know what the issue is."

I nod. "I guess."

"We could talk about options. IVF is certainly one of them. There are some more tests before we—"

"Can we think about it? I think I've had enough of tests for now." I meet Mark's gaze, and he nods.

"Of course." Doctor Faraday smiles. "Give my office a call when you want to talk further about it."

"Thank you."

It's a quiet drive home. Mark gives me space and time to think. He's been such a good partner to me, and Sophie adores him.

But we wanted to have a child together.

"Are you okay?" he asks as we pull into the driveway.

Lauren's car sits on the street outside—she picked Sophie up from school today while we went to our appointment. The only thing worse than being given bad news is the fact that she was so excited over the thought of us having a baby and we have to let her down.

I don't resent Mark—it's not his fault. I'm feeling miserable about the whole process. I haven't felt this down since the aftermath of the accident.

"I will be. Just need time and to work out what we do next."

He nods. "Let's put off talking about that for a while. Give ourselves some space."

"I like that idea."

Leaning over, he gives me a soft kiss. "Let's just go and spend an evening with our girl. Do you want to ask Lauren to stay for dinner?"

I nod. "Might as well. I was just going to order delivery. I'm too tired to cook tonight."

Mark gives my knee a squeeze. "Good thinking."

Together we walk into the house.

The television blares in the corner, but only Lauren sits on the couch.

"Hey, you two." She tilts her head and smiles.

"Hi. Where's Sophie?" I ask.

"In her room. She's got some story to write for school."

I take a seat on the couch next to her while Mark sits opposite.

"How did it go?" she asks.

"My sperm count is so low it might as well be non-existent."

Lauren frowns. "Are you okay?"

"We will be," I say. "Just need some time to wrap our heads around it."

"Yeah, I can imagine." She squeezes my arm. "I'm so sorry. Can they do anything about it?"

"There are options," Mark says. "But after all the tests, we decided to take a break before we think further about it."

She sighs. "I can understand that."

"Stay for dinner? I'm just going to order pizza or something."

Her eyes flash with happiness. "I'd love to."

She doesn't spend enough time with us. Mark worries about her living alone and her love affair with alcohol. She's always clear-headed when she has anything to do with Sophie—she loves her, so I do trust her.

But I also like to encourage her to spend time with us.

I like Lauren—she's a part of our family and not just because she's Mark's sister.

"I'll sort that out," Mark says. "The usual?"

I nod. We all have our favourites, and just for a moment I'm taken back to the night at Patrick's place with the tough steak and how he remembered what I liked. It's so weird how your memory sucks you in like that—from the best moments to the cringiest and the worst.

"Cassie?" Lauren gives me a nudge.

"Sorry, I was miles away."

"I said, if you need anything, just let me know. I want to be here for you guys while you're working through this."

I force a smile. "I appreciate it."

The couch dips beside me and arms wrap around my neck.

Sophie plants a big wet kiss on my cheek, and I roar with laughter before wiping it off with my hand.

She giggles. I love that sound.

Sophie leans her head against mine. "I'm glad you're home. What happened?"

She knows what's going on—it's impossible to keep anything secret in our house.

"Well, we have to stop and have a think about things because they're not working out the way we want." I squeeze her knee.

"Okay. You know I love you guys, right?"

"Of course I do."

"It doesn't matter if I'm an only child. I'm kind of used to it."

I meet her gaze—the one that always makes me think of her father. "You're very wise for your age."

"I learned from the best."

It's not easy being the mother of a teenager. No one ever warns you about how their puberty also hits you hard. Sophie's not a little girl anymore—she's a young woman who's beautiful and smart, and Mark always talks about how he wants to lock her in her room until she's twenty-one.

The thought of not having another child is hard, but as long as I have Sophie, I have everything.

———

THE FOLLOWING DAYS ARE TOUGH.

I've told Mark until I'm blue in the face that I don't blame him—how can I? It's not his fault that his body doesn't want to co-operate.

But he feels it to his bones.

He swore to never let me down, and he feels like he's betrayed that vow. It's ridiculous in my eyes, but he's also a proud man who's just been dealt a heavy blow.

He's quiet when he gets home, and I hate it.

Mark's the life of our family. It's not like him to be so withdrawn.

A week after our doctor's visit, we're still no closer to any resolution about what to do next, and after dinner with Sophie in bed, I join him on the couch.

His eyes have been filled with guilt since he got home. I know how to read him after all this time, and there's something he's holding back from me.

The only thing I'm sure about is that he's not cheating on me because he's been so steadfast in his love that hasn't wavered since the first night we spent together.

"What's happening with you? You're scaring me."

He meets my gaze. "There's something I need to tell you. You're not going to like it."

I swallow hard. The one thing I love about our relationship is our ability to communicate, but I'm not so sure right now.

"Tell me."

"A few weeks ago, I ran into an old friend of mine. He made me an offer—six months building work in Dubai at really good money, and I said no because I didn't want to be away from you and Sophie."

A lump forms in my throat. "Okay."

"I called him back today and told him that if it was still on the table, I'd be interested."

"Why?" I croak.

"Because I'm struggling with what's happened, and I know you are too. I thought maybe we could get away for a while—"

"When?"

"I'd leave in a week. There was more time to prepare but I said no originally, and now if I want the work, that's the timetable."

I close my eyes and grit my teeth. "You signed a contract."

"Yes." He grabs my hand and I open my eyes. "We need this, Cassie. Some time away from the mundane. Somewhere different."

I shake my head. "But we can't all go. Sophie has school and I have work."

"Can't you just take some time off?"

"With a week's notice?" I pull my hand away. "I'm used to you being impulsive, but usually it's things that benefit us. It sounds like the money is a good reason, but being away for six months? Now?"

He frowns. "I know. I just … I need to do something. I'm climbing the walls here feeling like I'm failing you."

I sigh. "You haven't failed me, Mark. It could have just as easily been me who had an issue. Even after having Sophie. The accident could have caused any kind of damage."

"But the doctor said—"

"What if on top of that there's something wrong with me that they just can't see easily? What if it doesn't matter what we do, *I* can't conceive?" I lean against him. "We're in this together. And now you want to run away from it all."

"Because it's making you miserable. I thought we could just get away."

I turn my head and look into his eyes. "I love you. But I can't just up and go. You can though. I mean, you have to if you've signed a contract. And you have staff you can put in charge here while you're gone."

"I'm sorry."

I shrug. "What's done is done. I can't stop it, can I?"

He grips my chin and pulls me closer. "I love you, Cassie. More than I ever thought possible. And when I'm back, we'll be able to build that extension onto the house you always wanted. I'm sorry I'm such a fuck-up."

I pull away and stand. "I'm just so angry at you. Why didn't you talk to me first?"

"You know me. Act and then think."

"Six months?"

He stands and wraps his arms around my waist. "So, I'm an idiot. But I did it for the right reasons. You have to know that."

"Of course I know that. Doesn't make me feel any better."

He holds me close, and I slip my arms around his neck. Being in his embrace always brings me comfort, but right now it feels like a band-aid for what's happened.

What the hell am I going to do?

18

CASSIE

I'm still so angry.

Mark took a job without any thought about me or Sophie.

And before I know it, he's on a plane and heading overseas.

Eight years as his partner and while I know he was thinking of the money, he never thought about the six months we'd have apart.

Sophie and I had no sooner got over the shock of him taking the job then he was off to Dubai, flying out a week after he signed the contract.

"My brother is an idiot." Lauren sighs before leaning her head on my shoulder.

It's the first night since he landed over there, and we're sharing a tub of ice cream in front of the TV.

"He is, but he means well."

She laughs. "You're so mad at him but still sticking up for

him. That's love."

I roll my eyes. "I'm hurt. But I know he didn't do it to hurt me. You know what your brother's like—he has to be the provider. And I've never expected that of him, but he can be a bit old fashioned like that."

Lauren straightens up. "It's my fault."

"What? Why?"

She shifts uncomfortably in her seat. "I think it's to do with when our parents died. Mark was never responsible. He dropped out of school, and he had a big falling out with Mum and Dad over it. I'm not sure we ever told you the full story about our parents dying."

"Not really. I know you moved in with him."

"He never liked talking about it. I was ten, and he was twenty. He left home when he was sixteen, and he became a builder's apprentice. He was nearly finished his apprenticeship when our parents went out one night to celebrate Dad's promotion at work. They never came home."

I gape at her. Mark's never shared the full story, and I respected his privacy. He has a lot of hang-ups about Lauren drinking and how responsible he feels for putting her on that track.

But he was a young man working through his own life issues while raising a child.

"Yeah. I woke up in the morning to Mark telling me that they died. I was glad for the age gap that we had between us because it meant that by Mark having a steady job he could take guardianship of me. But it put him in a role he wasn't really ready for. He's never said he resents it, but what twenty-year-old wants to take on a ten-year-old kid? He stepped up for me, but I always wondered if it meant he'd made sacrifices in his own life."

"He had to grow up earlier than he wanted to."

She nods. "I think he gets those old fuddy-duddy ideas because he had to be old before his time. But he never let me down. I can't pretend that our life has been perfect, and we've both done some really dumb things. But I always knew that he would be there to protect me. This is the longest he's been away from me since that night."

I tilt my head. "Come and stay here while he's away. I could do with the company, and it sounds like you could too."

"Maybe. I don't know if I'll stay the whole time, but I could stay some of it."

"I understand."

Lauren's also a free spirit which doesn't help Mark's anxiety about her. Apart from his unrealistic expectations around us being able to take the time to travel with him, I'm more than a little surprised he'd be okay with spending six months away from his sister.

"Do you ever think about Sophie's father?"

A lump forms in my throat. "Often. There's this look on her face that she gets when she's thinking hard—you know what a smart kid she is—and she looks so much like him. It's hard to ignore."

Lauren bites her bottom lip. "Do you think you'll ever tell him about her?"

There it is—the million-dollar question.

"I feel bad. I went looking for him once—Sophie was two months old. I should have told him then. But I was still so young and hurt and—"

"You loved him."

I nod. "And then I came home and had to have more surgery to rebuild my broken body. Anything that wasn't immediately necessary was delayed until after Sophie was born. I couldn't get rid of her though—she was my link to the life I lost. Not just Patrick's daughter, but the granddaughter my parents would never know."

She squeezes my arm.

"I've tried stalking him on social media. But he's got it locked up tight. So I stopped because I realised I didn't want to see him with a family that didn't include Sophie. And then life. It just …"

Lauren puts her spoon on the coffee table. "You had a lot on your plate."

"I did, but I could have told him. There are days when I have so much guilt over it, and then others when I feel like I can breathe because he doesn't know. What if I told him and he didn't want anything to do with her?"

"Oh, Cassie. Seriously, if that's how he reacted it would be his loss."

"You think I should tell him."

She shrugs. "I'd want to know. But I understand. It was a tough situation."

"It was, but how do I tell him now? 'Hey, here's your teenage daughter.' He'll hate me."

"Maybe. Maybe not. I'm glad she has Mark. I never thought I'd see him being a dad, but he adores her."

I smile. "He does. I'm so glad I met him. And you."

Her eyes glisten with tears. "Me too."

19

CASSIE

Mark's absence is felt.

He left a gaping hole in our lives—even if it's just temporary. If he'd been a man who worked away, we'd be used to it. But after eight years of his constant presence, his not being here for such a long stretch is difficult to get used to.

The house is quiet. It's the middle of term, so between school and after school activities, Sophie's wiped most nights. There's no booming laughter or late-night hot chocolate when Sophie should be in bed.

There's no sports on the TV during the weekend, with the hiss of a beer bottle being opened while Mark puts his feet up on the coffee table and I tell him off for the millionth time.

I miss him.

We talk several times a week, but I hate being alone in bed at night.

We're halfway through this ordeal when he calls. It's usually when Sophie's still awake so he can say goodnight to her, but this time it's late which rings alarm bells right away.

"Hey, babe."

I close my eyes. His voice is comforting, even though his tone is strained. He's probably tired—the days are long, but I'm sure he's counting the days until he comes home again.

"Hey, yourself. You sound tired."

There's silence for a moment. It's not like him. Even when he's tired, he makes time to speak to me, and that man is never short of a word.

"I'm on my way home. I'll be on the next flight out."

"What? Why?" I swallow hard. While I've hated him being away, I don't like the feeling he's lost his job.

"We'll talk about it when I get there. I just wanted to let you know I'm coming home."

We talked a few days ago, and he said nothing about this. *What's happened?*

"Mark? What's going on?"

"Look." His frustrated tone makes me grip the phone harder before he takes a breath. "Sorry, love. I know this is short and sudden, but I've got to get to the airport to get my flight. I love you, Cassie."

"I love you too."

"See you when I get there."

Tossing and turning all night, I don't get much sleep. What on earth is going on for Mark to be coming home halfway through his contract?

At best, I'm going to kill him for putting me through this worry.

At worst … I'm not even sure where to begin at worst.

I'm a wreck by the morning, and thankful that it's Saturday and I don't have to get up and go to work and get Sophie to school.

She bounces to the breakfast table—it's constantly amazing to me that kids have boundless energy for the weekend that they don't have during the week.

"Mum? Are you okay?"

I nod. "I just didn't sleep well. But I do have some news for you." Pausing, I take a sip of coffee. "Mark called me last night and he's on his way back."

"Dad's coming home?"

I nod. "Apparently. He was just about to leave for the airport."

"Are we going to pick him up?"

Shit. "I didn't ask. He didn't ask me to."

She frowns. "Did the job finish early?"

"I don't know, hon. Maybe. He didn't really give me much. I'm not sure which airline he's coming home on or the flight, so I'm not sure when he's arriving."

"That doesn't sound like him. I thought he'd want a party at the airport."

I laugh softly. "I'm sure he's just very tired. Let's be happy he's coming home. I'm sure he'll contact us again when he's closer."

———

IT'S after midnight the following day when Mark walks in the door.

Every hour since he last called me, the worst-case

scenarios have been running through my head—especially when it's been radio silence since then.

Of course I'm awake.

I've barely slept since that hurried call.

I close my eyes at the sound of a key in the door, and as the door clicks open and Mark walks in, I breathe a sigh of relief.

"Cassie? What are you doing up?"

I hold my palms to face the ceiling. "Oh, I don't know. I get this random phone call to tell me that you're coming home early and nothing since. What could possibly be causing me enough worry to stop me sleeping?"

He drops his bag where he's standing and makes his way to the couch, taking a seat beside me.

"I'm sorry."

"So, what is it?"

His brows pull together. "Can we just go to bed and talk in the morning? I feel like I've been flying forever."

"Please, Mark. Tell me what's going on."

He presses his forehead to mine. "Right now, all I want is a shower and to wrap myself around you. Can you give me that?"

Tears prick my eyes, but he's here and he's in one piece that I can see. Just that will help me sleep. "Fine."

I make my way to the bedroom and lie down in our bed.

After a quick shower, Mark strips and climbs in behind me.

He slips his arm over me and pulls me tight against him.

"You're the best thing that ever happened to me, Cassie Warren. You and our girl. I'm so glad to be home with you."

I'm not sure if I should be happy he feels that way or

worried that he's leading to bad news. Either way, he's clearly not going to open up.

I close my eyes, unsure if tonight will be any different to those while he's been away, but it doesn't take long when the warmth and comfort he brings help me sleep.

I'm out like a light.

———

It's after breakfast that he opens up.

Sophie's in her room watching a movie, and he waits until she's gone for a while before he walks into the kitchen and nuzzles my neck.

"We need to talk," he says softly.

A pit forms in the base of my stomach, but I nod and follow him into the living room where he pulls me down beside him on the couch.

"What's going on? You're really scaring me."

"I know. And I don't know how to tell you this."

I give him a short sharp nod.

"I … well … the past month, I've not felt right. So, I saw a doctor."

Oh God.

"I … I thought it was just the change in climate, but then I realised it's been going on a while. I just put it down to being tired after a long day and getting older. Didn't realise I'd lost weight either—you know I don't keep regular track. But it was down on my last doctor visit."

My throat tightens. "What is it?"

He pauses. The devastation on his face tells me it's something serious without him uttering a word. "I was diagnosed with melanoma. And it's metastasised."

"What?" I rasp.

His dark eyes are so mournful as he gazes at me. "It's terminal, Cass. We found it too late."

He wraps his arms around me while I weep on his chest. It's comforting, but nothing can prevent the gaping hole developing in my heart.

This isn't fair.

"How? How did we not pick it up when we saw the doctor for the fertility tests?"

He rubs my back. "Maybe because it wasn't what we were looking for? To be fair, the first lot of bloods they did weren't flash but they weren't terrible. They were thorough though and looked past that. I've had scans—the lot."

I pull away. "And that's it?"

Mark shakes his head. "No. I mean, I'll go and see my doctor and ask what else I can do, but the diagnosis was enough that I could get out of the rest of my contract and come home. They're certain about what it is."

"I guess we have to find out about treatments here. How we beat this?"

He frowns. "I think we have to prepare for the worst."

Tears roll down my cheeks. "How are you so calm?"

"Maybe because I've got a month's head start on this. I don't want to leave you, Cassie. Please tell me you know that."

I nod. "Of course I do."

"Mum? What's going on?"

My heart sinks at Sophie's voice.

Her gaze darts between Mark and me. Telling her is

going to break my heart—as if it's not already broken enough.

"Come here, love." Mark opens his arm to her, and she walks toward the couch, shooting glances at me.

We're about to break her heart.

She sits the other side of him, and he gives me a squeeze.

I look at him before shifting my gaze back to her. "Mark had to come home early because he's sick."

She frowns. "What do you mean sick?"

Mark gives her shoulder a squeeze. "Your mum's trying to say that I've been diagnosed with cancer."

"No." Her hands fly to her mouth, and her eyes swim with tears.

I've just hurt my child in a way I never, ever wanted her hurt. But there's no way to avoid it. She has to know.

"Come here." Mark opens his arms and Sophie falls into them. He hugs her tight, closing his eyes.

How long has he had symptoms he brushed off?

It makes me angry, but I can't be angry at him. He wasn't to know. It's not like he was in agonising pain and ignoring it.

I look up as he reaches for me, and the three of us are a weepy bundle on the couch.

How the hell do we tell Lauren?

After what feels like an eternity huddled together, Mark kisses me on the top of my head.

"I'm going over to see Lauren and tell her."

"Are you sure you want to do that alone?"

He nods. "I'll be gone a while. She's going to—"

"She'll need you. We have each other. But just remember, Mark, she has us too."

His brows knit. "I know. But I just need a little time with my sister."

"Okay," I whisper.

He gives us both a kiss and heads out the front door.

Sophie and I sit in silence for a while before she shuffles closer. "It's not fair. I don't know who my real dad is, and now I'm going to lose Dad."

I don't have any words. I've done this to my child. My life was a mess and while she's never spoken about it like this before, it's clearly had an impact.

She stiffens as I wrap my arms around her, but it's not long before she relaxes into me.

"I'm sorry, Mum. I know you must have your reasons. I'm just so upset about Dad."

"Me too, baby. Let's just see what's going to happen, okay? But I'm right here with you, and I always will be."

"I love you," she whispers.

"I love you too, Sophie Jane Warren."

She raises her head to look at me. "Am I like my bio dad?"

Tears prick my eyes. "Very much so."

"Will you tell him about me one day?"

"Of course I will."

She buries her face in my neck, and I close my eyes.

"I don't want Dad to die."

I don't have any more words, but I cradle my baby even as my shirt grows wet from her tears.

This isn't fair.

———

I'M CURLED around her in her bed when the front door opens and closes.

I press a kiss to my daughter's head and pull the blanket over her before watching her sleep a moment.

I'd do anything to take this pain away from her.

Mark's sitting on the couch when I enter the living room. "Sophie settled?"

I force a small smile and nod. "I stayed until she fell asleep. Haven't done that since she was little."

"I'm so sorry to do this to her." Mark buries his head in his hands.

I cross the room and drop onto the couch beside him. "You're not doing anything. It's not like you could help it."

He leans back on the couch. "I keep thinking of all the signs I ignored. How could I do that to you? How could I do it to us?"

Snuggling in against him, I press a kiss to his chest as he wraps an arm around me.

"If I'd thought you were ill, I would have made you go to the doctor. You can't blame yourself when there was nothing obvious."

"It could get rough from here on in. You know that, right?"

I sit up. "I'm not going anywhere."

He cups my cheek. "I know. You're too good a person to walk away from this. But I'll understand if you want to."

"What I want is a second opinion."

He nods. "I thought you might. I'll speak to the GP tomorrow. Maybe he can put an urgent referral through to the specialist."

"This can't be the end." I sniff.

Mark grasps my chin and pulls my gaze to him. "I love you, Cassie Warren. And if this is it, I want you to know I've had the best years of my life with you."

"How are you so strong?"

His lips curve into a sad smile. "One of us has to be. And I'll be that for you until the very end—whenever that is."

"Calm as well. I don't know how you're doing it."

His Adam's apple bobs as he swallows. "I can't fall apart. Not with Sophie here, and not around Lauren. Promise me that you'll always be there for her."

"Of course I will. You know how much I love her too."

"She's going to need it. I worry about her so much."

I give his hand a squeeze. "You wouldn't be you if you didn't."

20

CASSIE

A second opinion means a trip to Auckland.

I have so many questions swirling inside—questions I don't really want answers to.

Mark and I hold hands as we wait for his appointment. We didn't have to wait long given the severity of Mark's diagnosis, but every second counts where I'm concerned.

He seems more laid back which drives me insane but also makes me wonder if he knows more than he's letting on.

"Mark Burrows?"

We both look up to a man smiling kindly at us. I don't envy him his job. He must have to deliver awful news to people all the time. At least we already have the diagnosis.

All I can do is hope that he has better news.

"I'm sorry if you thought that I could give you a different diagnosis. Mark's cancer is very well advanced."

I nod. "I thought that might be the case."

"Would you like to talk some more about—"

"I want a word with the doctor alone. Why don't you go and grab a coffee or something? You must be starved," Mark says.

I switch my gaze between him and the doctor. Doctor Latimer gives me a sympathetic nod, and my throat tightens.

Mark wants to know how bad it really is.

I should be here.

I should know.

But maybe he also has questions he doesn't want to ask in front of me, and I should respect his privacy—no matter how hard it is to leave the room.

"Okay," I whisper.

He gives my hand a squeeze. "I'll come and find you when I'm done."

"There's a cafeteria in the main building, and some other food places if that helps," Doctor Latimer says.

"I'm sure I can find it." I give him a shaky smile.

"Thanks, babe."

I stiffen my spine and leave the room. It's not until I'm outside that I catch my breath and release a sob.

He's shutting me out.

I had a feeling that was happening, but now I know for sure.

Mark's trying to protect me. But we're supposed to be partners.

I walk across the road to the main building, and the signage guides me to the cafeteria where I order a latte and a scone.

I'm not really hungry but my stomach is all over the place and I need something to steady it.

And once I start eating, it turns out I'm ravenous.

I wolf it down and sip my coffee.

What's happening to us?

We've been solid for so long but the first time we hit a real roadblock, Mark starts freezing me out. It really began that day we found out his sperm count was low, but now? Now it's becoming even more obvious.

"Cassie?"

A deep voice shakes me out of my thoughts, and I look up into familiar blue eyes.

My throat tightens. *It can't be.* Not today.

"Patrick," I croak.

He gives me a tentative smile. "I … I wasn't sure I'd ever see you again."

"Same." I look back at the cup of coffee I've been cradling.

"Mind if I take a seat?"

I shrug. "Sure."

The heat of his stare makes my heart thud. He's the last person I ever expected to run into—at the worst possible time of my life.

The chair scrapes the lino floor as he pulls it out and drops onto it. "Are you okay? Your knuckles are white with how tight you're holding that mug."

I shake my head before meeting his gaze. "Why are you here?"

"I work here." His brows dip. "I'm a surgeon. I specialised in plastic—mostly doing reconstructions. What about you? I thought we'd be at uni together, but you never showed. Did you go to Otago?"

I blink back tears. It's not enough that I'm struggling with Mark's diagnosis—I've now got a living, breathing reminder of the past sitting in front of me.

It wasn't enough that Patrick cheated on me. The accident stole my future. I could have coped with university with a baby. But I couldn't cope with the grief of losing my parents, having a baby and the surgeries that followed.

My priorities shifted, and my dreams to become a doctor went flying out the window.

"No," I rasp. "I didn't go to uni in the end. I'm living in Hamilton."

He frowns. "But—"

"I'm sorry, Patrick, but I'm really not in the mood to reminisce. I'm here because my partner has been diagnosed with cancer and we're here for a second opinion."

His mouth falls open. "Shit, Cassie. Is he getting treatment?"

I shake my head. "It's metastasised Melanoma. He's going to die, and I can't do a damn thing about it."

He reaches over and grasps my shoulder.

I should hate him touching me, but I'm sitting in a strange place by myself while the man I love is talking to the doctor about his terminal illness.

"If there's anything I can do …"

Blinking back tears, I meet his gaze. "I just want to know how long I have left with him. It's so unfair."

"It is. I'm so sorry."

"Cassie, love?" Mark's voice takes my attention, and I shift my gaze to him as he walks toward the table. He shoots Patrick the side eye. "Are you okay?"

Patrick stands and turns toward him. "Hi, I'm Patrick Cross. I used to—"

Mark raises an eyebrow before holding out his hand to

shake. "I know who *you* are. Mark Burrows. Cassie's partner."

"I'm surprised you know who I am." Patrick glances at me.

"I know all about Cassie's past."

They're both silent for a moment, and I bite my bottom lip. "Mark? How did it go?"

"Not here." His smile feels forced. "Let's get to the hotel and we'll talk about it."

I swallow hard. It's not good. I can feel it in my bones. "Okay."

"How about I give you my details, and you call me if you need anything." Patrick grabs a napkin from the middle of the table and a pen from his pocket and jots down the number. "Any time. Day or night."

He holds it out to me, but I can't bring myself to take it.

Mark snatches it up. "Thanks, mate. Appreciate it."

He says nothing until we're back at the car, and I'm so staggered by today's events, I don't have anything to say either.

"Well, that was unexpected," he says as he turns the key in the ignition.

The engine roars to life.

We're staying the night in Auckland. Neither of us were sure we'd want to drive all the way home after our doctor visit.

Now all I want is to get to our hotel and lie down.

"You okay?" Mark asks.

I shrug. "It's been a day."

"I bet. Bit crazy to run into your ex." He snorts. "Life really is kicking me in the nuts."

I cross my arms and slouch into the chair.

"We'll be at the hotel soon."

"Are you going to tell me what the doctor said to you?"

He glances at me. "I asked about treatment options. What was available if anything."

I sit up. "And?"

"And I didn't want to upset you if the answer was no. But the answer was no. It's too far gone." He stops at a red light and looks at me. "I was going to wait until we were at the hotel to tell you because I know everything hurts right now."

I swallow down tears and nod.

"So let's get to the hotel and raid the minibar and order room service. I think we're owed that much."

21

PATRICK

Cassie Warren.

I thought of her over the years—telling myself I'd moved on. With no idea what I'd done to push her away, it was hard to get over that summer.

There have been other women in the past thirteen years, but no serious relationships. I couldn't do it—no one compared to Cassie.

Sad, but true.

Not that I had a lot of time for relationships anyway. I'd spent years studying and then throwing myself into my career. This year has been the big one—the one where I've gone into private practice, but I still operate at the hospital. It's busy, but not as hectic as the past few years have been.

It's a fulfilling career that I've worked hard for.

Part of the reason I pushed so hard—especially in the early days—was to forget about Cassie. My education suffered at first as a direct result of the aftermath of losing her. But I soon found my way by burying myself in the course work and doing better than I imagined.

I'm young to be doing what I'm doing, but after my mentor, Ethan, took me under his wing, I strode forward in leaps and bounds.

Tonight I get home and settle in for the night with pizza and a beer. Anything to try and distract me from having seen Cassie again.

It doesn't work.

It's a little after ten in the evening when my phone rings. While I'm available after hours for my patients, I don't often get calls with the nature of my work.

I don't recognise the number, but it could be someone from the hospital, so I answer. "Patrick Cross."

"Patrick. It's Mark Burrows. I was wondering if we could catch up and talk."

"Of course. When—"

"We're only here for the night. Staying in a hotel. Cassie's already asleep, so I thought I might come to yours or you could come to me."

I'm not sure what to say at first as he comes at me fast. "I'll come to you. Tell me where you're staying."

He gives me the name of the hotel—it's not too far.

"There's a bench out front. I'll wait there for you."

"Okay."

I head out to my car—relieved I had the sense to not drink more. The whole way my head is full of questions.

Why is he calling me?

I might have given them the number, but I didn't know if they'd actually call. If anything, I thought I'd still have to track them down. At least I know now she lives in Hamilton.

It would have been a good start.

What could he want?

I'm no good to him medically. I thought at one time about becoming an oncologist, but when I saw the difference that cosmetic surgery could make to people's lives, that decided my speciality. I often perform reconstructions, and I've removed melanoma before.

But Mark's cancer's far more advanced than anything I deal with.

I pull into the car park and find an empty spot near the door.

As I climb out of the car, a lone figure on a bench nearby waves me down.

I walk toward him, Mark studying me closely as I approach.

He nods. "Patrick."

"Mark." I take a seat on the bench beside him.

"I'm sure you're wondering why I called you."

Nodding, I knit my fingers together.

"I lied to her. I lied to my girl because she's already a mess and I can't tell her how bad it really is."

My lungs lose all air, and for a second I struggle to breathe. "What are you talking about?"

"The first doctor, in Dubai, said I have six months at best. The doctor here thinks it's half that."

I drop my hands. "Oh, shit, Mark. I'm so sorry."

"How do I tell her?"

"I don't know. Is there really nothing they can try?"

He shrugs. "He gave me a couple of options, but there are no guarantees and I would lose my quality of life. I want to spend every second I can with my girl and live our lives to the fullest." He grips his knees as if he's steadying himself for what he's about to say. "I'm glad it was you we ran into. She's going to need you."

I shake my head. "She's never needed me."

"You'd be surprised." He pauses. "I know all about you."

"What? How …"

"I don't want to talk about the past—I reckon you and Cassie can get into that later. But you were important to her once, and you might just be what she needs in the future."

I hold up my palms. "I'm lost."

"You two have history. And I need to know that she'll be okay when I'm gone. You can translate the medical jargon and be there for her when she needs you."

"I'm not sure you know what you're asking of me."

"I've been thinking about it since my diagnosis—who can be there for Cassie afterward? You'd already crossed my mind. I knew where you worked."

I frown. "Is that why you're here?"

"No. When I asked for a second opinion, my doctor referred me. Coming across you today was the icing on the cake."

Now I'm really confused. "What do you mean?"

"It saved me time hunting you down." He studies me closely, his dark gaze seeing right through me. "You and Cassie were always meant to be together—I'm sure of that. But maybe the time wasn't right, or things just didn't work out."

I close my eyes. "Mark, I'm not sure where you're going with this."

"I've loved that woman the past eight years, and I know she loves me. But there's a big part of her still tied up in you, and once you work that out, maybe you can move forward together."

I'm still puzzled by what he's asking, but I'm not about to pass up the chance to find out what happened all those years ago.

And today has just taught me that I never got over Cassie.

The moment I saw her, my heart kicked into overdrive. She's as beautiful as she ever was, and it broke me to see her so down.

I have so many questions about the past, and this is my chance to get answers.

22

CASSIE

After our trip to Auckland, Mark's health starts to obviously decline.

He stops working altogether—and I'm thankful again that I don't have rent or a mortgage to pay thanks to Gran.

He's tired.

It's so hard to see a man who was so full of energy when we met struggle to get through the day when he's not been doing much.

He still helps around the house—mows the lawn and takes out the rubbish—but the essence that made him Mark is rapidly disappearing and it hurts.

To make matters worse, Ian is on the scene.

They tend to drift apart and come back together—it's like a long running train wreck. Ian's toxic, and Mark keeps him at arm's length most of the time.

But as the fight goes out of him, he seems to want the people closest to him nearby, and I don't like it.

I've made that clear, but Mark's so focused on just getting through the day. So I do my best to stay out of the way.

When there's a knock on the door one Friday afternoon, I roll my eyes, take a deep breath, and open it.

It's not Ian.

I swallow hard.

Patrick's blue-eyed gaze drinks me in. Sophie inherited that intensity—the kind that makes you want to spill all your secrets.

"Patrick? What are you doing here?"

He shoots a glance over my shoulder at Mark, and my heart sinks.

"Mark invited me for the weekend. I've changed my schedule so I can spend time with him."

I raise my eyebrows and shift my gaze to Mark. "Mark?"

"I thought you might appreciate some help, love. Patrick can answer any medical questions we have and I know I'm not as helpful as I was."

"Do you really think *that* matters to me?"

"Who was at the door?"

Sophie bursts into the room, and I freeze.

The moment Patrick sees her will be burned on my brain for the rest of my life.

Her eyes widen, and she looks at me.

I shoot a glance at Patrick. His jaw is set, his eyes fixed on Sophie's face.

"Sophie. This is Patrick. He's an old friend of your mother's." Mark swoops in, and relief floods my system because I don't know if I could have found the words.

"Hi." She breathes out loudly, and I know, oh God I know.

That's the effect he has on women. She's going to hate me when she finds out he's her father.

"He's staying with us for the weekend." Mark meets my worried gaze. "Patrick's a doctor, too. So if we've got any questions, he's here to help with those."

She nods before shifting her gaze back to me. "What's for dinner?"

"I'm going up the road for fish and chips soon. Want to come for a ride?" Mark asks.

Sophie beams. "Yes. Can I get a donut?"

He chuckles. "You can get whatever you want, sweetheart."

"Thanks, Dad."

Patrick seems to deflate at her words, but I can't cope with this right now. It's difficult enough having him in my house—what on earth is Mark thinking?

"I guess you'd better come in." I motion for Patrick to move forward, and he steps through the door, gym bag in hand.

"You didn't know?" he asks.

I shake my head. "No. It's a surprise."

"Not an unpleasant one, I hope."

Mark moves out of the corner of my eye, and I glance at him as he watches Patrick and I interact. What was he thinking?

"Just unexpected."

Mark grabs his car keys and pecks me on the cheek. I give him a look as if to say, 'I'll talk to you later.'

"Come on, Soph. Let's go and get dinner."

We stand in silence as the two of them leave the house, Sophie giving Patrick one last look before she goes.

The door closes with a soft click.

"I'm sorry if you weren't expecting me. Mark really wanted me to come, and I couldn't say no given the circumstances. If you want me to go and stay in a hotel, I will."

I let out a sigh. "No, it's fine. We've got a spare room and if having you around makes him happy, I can make it work."

"How's he doing?"

His question catches me by surprise. I was sure the first thing out of his mouth would be something about Sophie, but I'd rather talk about Mark than the past right now so it doesn't upset me.

"Slowing down. I think it's worse than he's letting on, but he's a proud man."

Patrick nods. "I got that impression."

Tears prick my eyes. "I don't know what to do. I feel so useless."

He wraps his arms around me, and I surrender to it. I hate having him here, but the comfort he's bringing me right now counteracts that feeling.

"You're not useless. You love him and you see what's happening. But I'm here now, and I'll be here whenever you need me."

"I don't want to disrupt your life." I raise my gaze to meet his.

He should be angry with me, and I should be angry with him. But I'm so damn tired of feeling like my world is about to end and having no one to talk to. Sophie's too young, and Lauren's dealing with the impending loss of Mark in her own way.

"You're not. I spoke to Mark not long after I saw you at the hospital, and we discussed me coming down for weekends or when I can squeeze in time. I've just spent the past few weeks rearranging my schedule so I can be here. If it's okay with you, I'll be here Friday afternoons and leave on Sundays. Longer toward the end."

I bite my bottom lip. Do I want this? Does it matter? If Mark needs Patrick to be here …

"Okay. I'll talk to Mark. You two blindsided me with this."

"I did wonder." He pauses. "I was blindsided by your daughter."

I nod. "I'm sure."

"But right now the priority is Mark. I have plenty of questions, but I don't want to make this time any more stressful for you and your family."

"Thank you."

He loosens his grip. "I can see you're tired, and probably stressed to hell, so anything I can do to help, please just ask."

"Are you telling me I look bad?" I crack a smile. It's hard not to. My worlds are colliding and I can't stop it, but the weight is off my chest with him not asking questions.

"You haven't looked bad a day in your life. You're still gorgeous."

My cheeks heat up. I know he's lying, and he looks like someone who stepped out of a clothing catalogue just the way he always has.

"Stop it."

"It's true." His eyes dance with mischief.

"Patrick, you can't talk to me like this."

"Who's going to stop me?"

I pull myself away from him and shake my head. "I'm pretty sure Mark didn't invite you here to flirt with me."

"Maybe I have a lot of catching up to do." He grasps my

forearm. "Besides, it's got you smiling, and that's something Mark does want."

"It's just so hard."

"I know it is. But I've got you, Cassie. For however long you need me."

I raise my hand over my mouth to try and stop myself from bursting into tears. Since the day Mark told me about his diagnosis, I've felt so alone.

The last person I want to lean on is standing right in front of me. But to hear him say he's got me is everything. It's exactly what I need at the right time.

"Hey," he says softly. "It's okay to let go. That's why I'm here. I know you're carrying a big burden, but you never have to do it alone."

My shoulders slump, and he pulls me into his arms. I close my eyes and draw on his strength as he holds me tight.

I don't know if I could ever trust him with my heart again, but in this moment, I trust him to back me up and be there for me.

"Thank you," I whisper.

"You don't have to thank me. I'd do anything for you."

Except be faithful.

That's the past, and this is a whole different life. Now he's back, and it seems like he's made some promise to Mark. I'll be asking Mark about that when I get a chance.

I'm not sure how long we stay like that—me wrapped in Patrick's arms—but we fly apart when the front door opens and Mark walks in.

His gaze hits me and while in the past he would have narrowed his eyes at any man that close to me, he's calm. A small smile plays on his lips.

"Who's hungry?" he asks.

"I am." Sophie bounces in the door behind him. "I'll get the plates."

Mark takes the bundle of fish and chips to the dining table and opens the paper. The scent of the food wafts through the room, and it's bizarrely comforting.

"Everything okay?" Mark asks.

"Fine," I snap.

He holds up his palms. "How about we eat and then talk?"

"No one likes you when you're hangry, Mum," Sophie says.

I can't help it—I laugh, and before I know it, she's laughing too while Patrick and Mark look at us like we're nuts.

She places the plates on the table, and we all gather around and help ourselves. As usual, Mark's gone overboard. There's nothing he likes better than having a late-night snack of reheated fish and chips.

And as we usually do on Fridays, we sit in front of the TV with our plates. It's usually relaxing, but as Patrick takes a seat across from the couch, tension builds in my shoulders.

Sophie sits on the floor. It's her usual spot. By the time we watch a movie, she's stretched out and has usually got her pillow from her bed so she can lie down comfortably.

She fixes her gaze on Patrick, and my heart sinks.

"So, you knew Mum when she was young?"

He nods. "I did. We grew up together."

Sophie's brows knit. "Why haven't I met you before?"

My mouth goes dry.

Patrick shrugs. "We went our different ways. I became a doctor, and now I'm surgeon." He shifts his gaze to me. "I need to catch up with your mother to find out what she got up to."

"She's a store manager," Sophie says.

"She is?" His gaze hasn't moved off me.

Sophie nods, her ponytail flying. "That's where she met Dad. He's not my bio dad, but he lets me call him that because he moved in with us when I was a kid."

A bemused smile plays on Patrick's lips. "When you were a kid, huh?"

Her grin lights up the room. "You know what I mean."

Patrick chuckles. "Yeah, I do."

Mark grabs my hand, and I look at him. He shoots me a wink as if to reassure me that everything's okay. He knows how to read me so well.

I might not be saying much, but I'm falling apart inside.

This was what we were supposed to have before our lives were derailed by Patrick's actions. Despite the years, and Mark's love, I can't pretend it doesn't hurt.

And now watching father and daughter together—interacting as if none of it got in the way—is tough.

I love Mark.

I loved Patrick.

And more than anything, I love this girl who's laughing and joking with the man she doesn't realise is her bio dad.

I really don't know how to handle this.

———

AFTER DINNER AND TWO MOVIES, Mark and Sophie take care of the limited dishes while I show Patrick the spare room.

"Spare towels are in the hall cupboard if you want a

shower, and there are more pillows in the wardrobe." I point everything out and turn to leave.

"Cassie."

I hesitate. For so long I've thought about seeing him again, and this is nothing like I thought it'd be.

"For what it's worth, I'm sorry that you didn't know I was coming. Mark's a bit light on detail."

I turn back. "The way he's been acting lately, I'm not really surprised about that."

"He loves you. Your daughter was a surprise."

My throat constricts.

"She's a lot like you—like you were at her age. Whatever that is."

"I'm really proud of her."

"So you should be. I'm looking forward to spending more time with all of you. If that's okay."

The tension eases a little. He's not pushing anything—not yet. But I'll take what I can get.

"If that's what Mark wants—"

"What about you? What do you want?"

He takes a step closer, and my breath hitches.

"I just want my life back."

"I understand that. I'm here to try and help you where I can. I do care, you know."

"Thank you." I take a step backward.

"What about your parents? Where are they in all of this?"

My throat tightens.

The memory of them dying is tied so closely to his betrayal and leaving. I don't think about that now—it leads to other conversations I'm not ready to have.

"I'd rather not talk about them right now. How about I let you get comfortable?"

He studies me a moment before giving me a short, sharp nod. "Sounds good."

Sophie's not with Mark when I get back into the kitchen, and he meets my gaze and nods toward the hallway. "She's gone to bed."

"I'm just going to head there now."

He studies my expression. "I'll join you after I've locked up."

I'm so on edge that I'm not quiet as I stamp my way to the bedroom and close the door. After stripping off, I pull a nightgown over my head and slide into bed.

I don't know what Mark is thinking, but I wish he'd just talk to me.

He joins me a few minutes later, gently closing the door behind him and undressing.

"What is he doing here?" Anger builds inside me—the first opportunity to let it since Patrick got here.

Mark holds up his palms in surrender. He pauses a moment before climbing into bed with me.

I cross my arms and stare at the wall, ignoring him.

"You two have unfinished business," he says.

"Maybe, but it was up to me to make that decision, not you."

He tugs on my arm, and I slowly unfold them—still angry, still not looking at him. I'm afraid if I do, I'll really lose the plot.

"Come on, Cassie, love," he says softly.

I let out a sigh. There's no way I can stay angry at him forever, not when we don't have much time left.

Letting him pull me into the bed, I slide down beside him.

He cups my cheek, gazing into my eyes. "I love you, Cassie. You're the love of my life. But I've known the whole time that I'm not yours."

I search his eyes. "That's not—"

"It is. I think it's possible to love more than one person, and you do because you have the biggest heart I've ever had the fortune to meet. And whether you like it or not, like I said before, you two have unfinished business."

I drop my gaze. Mark has always been honest to a fault, and usually it doesn't hurt the way it does now. "I'm just not sure how to deal with all of this."

"None of us do. I'm trying to make the best of an opportunity that I saw open. Just the way I did when I first laid eyes on you." He chuckles softly. "The minute I saw you, I thought, I'll have me some of that."

I laugh, despite feeling like I'm dying inside.

"And then I was lucky enough that you let me in. You let me be the father to that beautiful girl and the partner of the most wonderful woman in the world. But I can't stop what's happening, and I can either fight what's inevitable afterward or make sure that the two women I love more than anything on this planet are taken care of when I'm gone."

Tears well in my eyes. "Who said it's inevitable?"

"I saw the way he looked at you. And I don't blame him because that's the way *I* look at you. And if I can give you that after I'm gone, and give Sophie her dad, then I'll have made sure that you're okay."

I sniff. "I should have told him a long time ago."

He nods. "Yes, you should have. But I understand why you didn't, and I understand why *this* life became so important to you. Because we've been happy, maybe happier than I ever deserved to be."

"I love you," I choke out.

"I know you do, love. So please respect what I'm asking you and give the man a chance. You don't have to tell him about Sophie yet. I think he's smart enough to work that one out for himself. But let him spend time with us, so he can get to know his daughter and be the strength for you that I can't be."

He wraps his arms around me, and we lie in silence for a while.

"I hate this. All of it," I whisper.

"Me too. But this is the hand we were dealt and we should make the most of what time we have left."

"How did you get to be so wise?"

He snorts. "Alcohol and bad decisions in the past. But the best thing I ever did in life was fall in love with you. You and Sophie changed me for the better—you have no idea how much. And I'm so sorry I can't continue on this journey with you. But I don't think I could ask for anyone better to join you on it than your daughter's father."

Tears spill onto my cheeks, and Mark wipes them away with his fingers.

"The thought of leaving you is hard enough, Cassie. Give me this, okay?"

"Okay." I swallow down my resentment.

"Let's get some sleep. I'm not getting any younger."

I bark out a laugh as he holds me tighter.

I'm not sure sleep will be as easy for me as it is for him, but when I close my eyes, surrounded by him, it's not really difficult at all.

23

PATRICK

The weekend was crushing in so many ways. When I suggested supporting Mark, of course I had an ulterior motive. It meant getting close to Cassie, maybe finding out the answers to some of the questions I've had for years.

Instead, I've realised that the situation is even tougher than I thought. I knew what Mark told me, of course. But when we had our initial conversation, he'd just had some bad news. People take news all kinds of ways—it was hard to tell how he took his because he seemed more focused on Cassie.

But he's not a well man, and I can see how stressed that makes Cassie. She's not as naive as he thinks she is. And she's wound up like a spring.

I could hammer her about the past, and about my new questions regarding Sophie. I don't know anything about her. When was she born? How old is she? But I just have this feeling. If Cassie and I had a child, I think she'd look like Sophie.

But there's is a gap in my knowledge about Cassie. I know everything about her up until that day that something went wrong. I know nothing of the time we've been apart. Thirteen years is a long time. Feelings change, and I thought despite not moving on with anyone else that that was just me and not related to the break-up I had with Cassie.

Seeing her again has triggered all those memories and my need to know what happened. She slipped through my fingers, and she's always been the one that got away. Being around her has reminded me of what I fell in love with. She's beautiful, smart, funny, and it's clear she's a good mother to her daughter.

Mark's obviously dedicated to both of them, and I'm glad she found someone good to take care of her. Which makes this whole situation even harder because she's about to lose that.

I'm torn between this jealousy I have over the feeling that he took my life and the knowledge that he's about to lose it all.

So I need to let this play out, because if I put any pressure on Cassie now she'll only resent me and I might lose everything all over again.

"You're moody today," Ethan says.

"Today's a big day. We've got this transfer of this patient from me to you, and I've just had a really big weekend."

I've told Ethan all about what's happening. As soon as Mark spoke to me, I needed someone to talk to. And Ethan's probably the best friend that I have. He's older than me, sure, but he's a good listener.

"How did it all go?"

"Mark is sicker than he's letting on. Cassie's not dealing

with it very well, but he's doing his best to reassure her that everything will be okay. I'm going to be there for them. It won't be easy, but if it's okay with you, I'll reduce my workload over the next few months so that I can be there."

He nods. "You're a good man. I wouldn't expect anything less from you."

"There's something else. Cassie has a daughter. I didn't want to probe with too many questions while she's struggling with all of this. I don't know the kid's exact age, but I think it fits. What if she's mine?"

Ethan fixes his gaze on me. "Then she'll still be yours in the future after Mark dies. I think you're doing the right thing holding back."

I swallow hard. I already know that, but it doesn't make the whole situation easier.

"If she is, I just don't get why Cassie would keep that from me."

He shrugs. "When the time comes, hear her out. If that's what she did, she must have had her reasons."

I run my fingers through my hair. "I never got answers about why she dumped me in the first place. Something happened at that party, but I don't know what."

He gets up from his desk and walks around it before joining me on the couches. "You've waited this long, what's a bit longer?"

"I guess."

"Look." He knits his fingers as if he's about to impart the pearls of wisdom I'm used to from this man. He's been my mentor for eight years now, and I'm so grateful for the man who not only recognised my talent but nurtured it and now treats me as his equal. "You know where she is now. And you said that she's open to you being around. I think you should stick with it and see where it goes. You'll get your answers."

"Thank you."

"For what?"

"For saying what I needed to hear."

He smiles. "That's what I'm here for. Now, we really need to talk about today."

There is a patient who's been seeing me for a while and Ethan is taking over her care today. She's young—still a teenager—but a couple of years ago, the apartment she was in caught fire and the alarms had been deactivated by one of her flatmates who were sick of the sound of a flat battery beeping.

Emily was lucky to escape with her life, but not before she sustained significant burn injuries. I've performed several skin grafts, but there's been a gap in between surgeries to allow healing. So, her treatment has dragged on.

But along the way, she developed an unhealthy interest in me. Despite there only being one surgery left, Ethan and I decided that he would take over her care. Her parents have been with her the whole way, so we've discussed it with them first and they've agreed to support the change. They'd also noticed changes in her behaviour when it came to me.

She's been talking about work she doesn't need to extend our time together, and I'm not the type to take advantage like someone else might.

"I'll introduce myself and you take a back seat. If she wants an explanation then you can give her one, but I think her exposure to you should be limited to that and then you leave and I'll take the consult," he says.

I nod.

"I'd suggest you staying out of it altogether, but I think you being present at first might ease any tension. And you can graciously dip out when I explain that she has no other option."

I swallow hard. I'm glad for Ethan's guidance when it comes to these things. While I've been a doctor for several years now and I'm confident in my abilities including dealing with people, it's good to know he has my back.

He gives me a reassuring smile. "We've got this, Patrick. It happens. You know she'll be safe with me."

"I know. I just hate this whole situation."

Ethan grips my shoulder and gives it a squeeze. "We'll also look at your schedule and see what else I can take on while you're dealing with this whole Mark situation."

"Thanks, Ethan."

"You're a good man, Patrick. Don't forget that."

When I'm back in my office with the door closed, I take a deep breath and shut my eyes. I've heard stories about patient attachment but never had to deal with something like this before. But then again, most surgeries are a one off and after they're complete and the final check-up is done, I never see the patient again.

I trust Ethan, and in all honesty, I have far bigger things on my mind right now.

When Emily and her parents arrive, we usher them into Ethan's far bigger office. They sit on his couch, and he sits opposite. I position myself, as planned, by his desk farther back. It's important for him to take the lead on this from here on in.

Emily glances between me and Ethan. It's clear she doesn't trust what's going on.

"I'm glad you're all here today. I'd like to talk about Emily's surgery," Ethan starts.

"Why?" Emily asks.

Ethan glances at me.

"Dr Stone will be taking over your case. He'll be doing the last of your surgeries," I say.

Her eyes are wild as her mother tries to reach for her hand.

"But you're my doctor."

"Honey," Mrs Shaw says. "This is for the best. There's only one surgery to go—"

"Patrick is my doctor. I want him."

Ethan leans forward. "Dr Cross is unable to perform your surgery. We've got the date scheduled, so to keep that, I'll be stepping in. I understand this might be distressing, but I can assure you that you'll be well taken care of."

She shakes her head. "No. I don't want to do it."

"Dr Stone is my mentor. He taught me everything I know. You're in safe hands." I give her what I hope is a reassuring smile.

"But—"

"Emily. We really need to get you in as scheduled. Let us talk about it." Ethan gives me a nod, and that's the signal for me to step out of the room.

I'm out of here for the day—this was my last appointment. Knowing this was coming up, I made plans to take my mind off it.

I don't visit my parents often.

When we first moved to Auckland, I lived with them, but when Dad retired early, they moved out west toward the coast. It's a decent drive out there—long enough that I don't just pop out to visit.

But I told my mother I'd be there for dinner—I wasn't sure how this afternoon would go and thought I might need some moral support.

I'm tired, but I'd like to see them.

When I pull into their backyard, it's nearly 6.30 p.m., and the sun is setting.

The scent of roasting chicken floats out the open door.

Mum's standing at the oven, peeping in when I step inside.

"Hope I'm not too late."

She closes the door and turns toward me, smiling as she opens her arms. "You're just in time."

I hug her tight and kiss the top of her head.

Dad appears in the doorway, and I let go of Mum and make my way to him. He grabs my hand and pulls me in for a hug.

"Let me get dinner served and we'll eat," she says. "You must be starving."

"I am now I can smell it. I haven't had roast chicken in ages."

Dad chuckles. "You need to come out here more often."

Holding up my palms, I shift my gaze between them. "Okay. I get the message."

It doesn't take long before all the food is on the table, and we eat in silence. There's a lot to say, but I think Mum and Dad appreciate that it's been a long day for me and I just want to stuff myself silly.

There's time for talking afterward.

Dad volunteers to wash the dishes while Mum and I sit in

the living room. The television drones on in the background while she picks up her knitting.

I don't want to talk about today, but I do have other things I need to get out.

"I've been thinking about Cassie lately."

Mum puts down her wool, her eyebrows raised. "I thought that was all in the past. The way she treated you ..."

"Something went horribly wrong, and I think I need to find out."

Mum frowns. "After all this time? Has something happened?"

Do I tell her? Or will it give her false hope if it turns out that Sophie's not mine?

"She's just been on my mind a lot lately."

She grips my bicep. "She hurt you so badly. What happens if you find her and she's happily married with children? She's moved on, Patrick, and you need to too."

I nod. "I know."

"I love you. That time of your life was so bad, and I don't want to see you hurt like that again."

Her face is full of the tension I feel talking to her about this.

"I'm sorry, Mum. I don't want to upset you."

She smiles, but it feels forced. "Then let's not talk about this again."

I nod. "I should get going."

"Come and stay for longer next time. Maybe stay for a weekend."

"We'll see." My throat tightens. "I'm ... I'm supporting a friend of mine who has terminal cancer. So, I'll be travelling to stay with him at weekends for the foreseeable future."

Her brows knit. "Oh? I'm so sorry."

"It's so awful, Mum. He's got a partner and a daughter who adore him. But they found melanoma too late, and he's not got a lot of time left."

She pulls me into a hug, her knitting abandoned, and I let her. While she might still have strong views on Cassie, when she knows who I'm spending time with, I'm sure she'll understand given the circumstances.

Meanwhile, I'll stay again this weekend and see how things go.

Maybe now isn't the time to hit Cassie with questions, but I will get to the bottom of this.

No matter what.

24

PATRICK

Cassie's always cold when I first get to the house.

I don't blame her. Whatever happened in the past, she's clearly not as comfortable with me being around as Mark is. Sophie's her usual bouncy, happy self. Whatever is going on with Mark isn't getting to her.

But I think most of that is because of the way she's being parented.

Mark and Cassie both put her first. And maybe that's the way it should be, because the once vital man—even the version I met—is going downhill. And there's nothing that any of us can do to stop it.

So I'm sticking it out because apart from the fact that I still have feelings for Cassie, I want to be here for both Sophie and for Mark. He's a decent man—a family man. And whether or not this is supposed to be my family, he's taken good care of them up until now.

He still would be if it wasn't for this awful illness that will take him away from all of us. It would be the easiest thing in the world to resent him, but I can't bring myself to do that because he's the one saying goodbye.

Cassie gives me the side eye as Mark asks for two beers from the fridge. Whatever he has been doing around the house has been abandoned, and when I'm here I try and pick up what I can. The last thing I want is for Cassie to carry that whole burden.

She brings them in, and he rips the caps off with a bottle opener attached to his keyring. And then he hands one to me, giving me a steady look that tells me that we're about to have a conversation that might not be too comfortable.

We've had a few of those lately. He's never directly addressed anything about Cassie and my past, and I've been wondering when that will come up because no doubt it will.

Cassie calls for Sophie and makes her excuses to head to the supermarket. At least it'll give us time to talk.

"She's a good girl that one," Mark says as Sophie follows her mother out the door. "Sophie, I'm talking about."

I nod. "She is. She reminds me a lot of her mother when she was younger."

Mark studies me closely. "I think you know the truth, but you're too afraid to ask her."

I nod. "I don't want to add to the stress she's already under."

He takes a long draw of his beer. "That's how I know you'll be good for her. I reckon you'll work things out when the time is right."

My throat tightens. "I wish you wouldn't talk like that."

Mark chuckles. "The sooner I'm gone, the sooner you can sweep her off her feet. Give her the life she was supposed to have with you."

"You know saying this is fucked up, right? Do I need to get you a psych check-up?"

He laughs even harder before growing serious. "I know it is. But I love that woman so damn much, and I hate that I didn't see the signs of this until it was too late. So I'm doing my best to give her the happy ending she deserves."

"You're a good man."

"I wish I'd been a better man."

I frown. "Mark, you've given her love for the past eight years. Sophie too. And stability. The reason she's so broken up about this is not only because she loves you, but you've been their rock."

"That's why I need you to be here." He looks down at his drink. "Cassie's so strong. She had to be everything to that girl when I met her. But she's also soft and vulnerable. She's going to be a mess after I'm gone."

I swallow hard. "I'll be here for them."

"My sister will struggle, but I don't know how to help her. You, I got lucky with." He chuckles again. "But I hope you and Cassie will do what you can for Lauren."

"Anything. Anything you need."

He studies me closely. "You're a good man. You could have walked away from this and waited until I was gone, but you're here and that counts for something."

"I couldn't walk away." I take a sip of my drink and put the bottle down on the coffee table. "I've trained my entire adult life to take care of people, and I couldn't ignore what you're going through. So I'll be here when I can, and it's not just about Cassie."

"Think we can be friends?"

I smile. "I think we already are."

25

CASSIE

It all happens so fast.

We have weeks rather than months—that much is clear.

Mark's been moved under palliative care. We have a caregiver who comes in once a day to make sure his needs are taken care of, which means I don't worry as much while I'm at work.

It also means if anything happens, he's not going to hospital. We have a letter from the GP for the paramedics telling them to make him comfortable instead.

I hate it, but I couldn't argue.

It's what Mark wants. And I get it. If they'd only found his cancer earlier then things might be different.

Juggling everything is difficult but having Patrick with us over weekends is more helpful than I'll ever admit.

He's getting closer to us—it can't be helped. But my

head's still so full of everything happening with Mark that I can't face talking to him about Sophie.

That can wait until I'm ready.

Although, from the amount of time he spends with us, he has to have worked it out a long time ago. I just don't have the emotional strength to deal with it.

Mark gets weaker by the day. He's still mobile, but struggling. It's so hard to watch, but we all do our best to keep optimistic.

Lauren worries me. She floats in and out and gets less focused every time we see her. In the past, when Mark was concerned, he'd track her down and talk some sense into her. But that's not something he's capable of doing anymore, and she gets defensive if I try.

It's become a normal weekend for Mark and Patrick to be in front of the television watching some sport. They've become friends which is weird.

I'm not as resentful as I first was about Mark inviting Patrick to spend time with us. But I do what I can to avoid speaking to Patrick alone. If Mark wants to have a close friend he can trust in his final days, that's all well and good. But there's still so much to deal with when it comes to Patrick and me.

I have so many regrets. Mark and I never married. Never even really talked about it. We were just content to be together and that was that. I'm sad that we never got to have a baby together.

I know he would've been a good dad—he *is* a good dad to Sophie.

It hurts and I'm bottling it all up for Mark's sake.

It's not good for me but I can't let go of it or I'll fall apart, and Sophie needs me to be strong.

The only moments I allow myself to weaken are when I know Patrick has my back—he's stepped in and bought dinner more than once to give me a break.

It's been three months since we ran into him at the hospital. Almost three months of him arriving on a Friday night and leaving Sunday afternoon. It's become as routine as everything else around here.

Standing in the dining room, I rake my fingers through my hair. I'm tired—this whole thing is exhausting—but I want as much time as possible with Mark. Sophie's tucked herself away in her room. She seems to do that more often these days, but I think she's mourning what's to come in her own way.

"You should go and take a nap, love," Mark calls from the living room. "You look like you're asleep on your feet."

Patrick turns to look at me. "I've got this. Take a break."

I shake my head. "I'm fine."

"Cassie, I really need you to go," Mark says.

I frown, and Patrick shifts his gaze to Mark. "What's going on?"

"I don't want her to see this."

"See what?" I cover the distance between rooms and circle the couch until I'm facing him.

His breathing's laboured, but he's doing what he can to hide it.

"Mark?" I drop onto my knees in front of him.

"Mark, mate. Tell me what's happening." Patrick's got his attention fully focused on him now.

He raises his hand to his chest. "It hurts here."

"What about your left arm?"

"That too."

Patrick nods. "Do you want me to call an ambulance?"

Mark nods.

"What's happening?" I ask.

Patrick doesn't answer but takes my hand in his and gives it a squeeze as he brings his phone to his ear.

Once he's done, he turns to me. "If I had to guess, I'd say Mark appears to be having a cardiac event. The paramedics will be here soon and can give him some pain relief."

"Pain relief? But what if …"

"Cassie," Mark grunts. "Come and sit with me."

Even though my feet are concrete, I push myself up and sit beside him. Any colour has gone from his face now. In a matter of weeks, the life has drained out of him, but I see it more than ever now.

It's breaking my heart.

He raises his hand to his chest again and grimaces.

"They'll be here soon, and we'll get some answers." Patrick directs the words to me, but he doesn't have to try to reassure me.

I know what this means—I know there's no coming back.

Whether this is a heart attack or not, the only thing they will do is make him comfortable. They'll do what they can to stop the pain, but it's still happening.

Mark's dying.

A siren echoes in the distance. They're coming but there's a part of me that wishes they'd take him to hospital.

But we're past that point.

Patrick places his hands on my forearms. I blink a bunch of times before I meet his gaze, and I nod. I let him help me to a nearby chair and sit.

He takes care of everything.

He goes to the door and lets the paramedics in.

He shows them the GP's letter.

"We've got some medication to help make you comfortable, okay?" The female paramedic smiles, and Mark nods. "Did you want to stay on the couch, or can we help you to bed?"

"I'd just like to lie here if I could."

I swallow hard.

He's going to die right here in the living room.

His gaze hits mine. "Cassie? I don't—"

"I'm not leaving."

He nods, and they administer the medication.

Patrick rushes around gathering pillows to prop him up, and Mark's eyelids flutter.

They stand back to give him room, and Patrick takes hold of my hand. I stare up at him.

"How about we sit you next to him?"

I let him guide me toward the couch where he's pulled up a kitchen chair.

I take Mark's hand in mine.

The drugs work fast. He smiles through the haze.

"I love you," I whisper.

It takes a few more moments before he closes his eyes. We seem to sit like this forever, until Patrick grips my shoulder.

"He's gone, Cassie. I'm so sorry."

"Where's Sophie?"

"I'm right here."

I turn my head and Sophie's tucked into a chair, her knees pulled up. She comes to me when I wave her over, and I hold her tight.

She's the one who cries.

All I feel is numb.

"Cassie? Where's the number for your GP? Is he the one coming to take care of the details?"

I nod.

Patrick presses a kiss to my forehead. "I've got this. You just take care of Sophie."

When she's all cried out, I lead her to her room and curl up on her bed until she falls asleep. It's the middle of the afternoon, but I think any semblance of normality is gone today.

It's Patrick who deals with the GP and the death certificate details.

It's Patrick who calls the funeral director.

It's Patrick who organises the pick-up.

He's waiting next to the couch when I come back out and make my way to him.

"Is it done?" I ask.

He nods. "They'll be here as soon as they can. Is Sophie okay?"

I shake my head. "Not right now, but she will be."

He reaches over and takes my hand. "How about you?"

"Same?"

"I'll make some coffee. Want me to call Lauren?"

Oh God. Lauren. She'll be devastated.

"Hey," he says. "You're not alone. I can go and pick her up if you want me to."

I shake my head. "I'll call her. I'm not even sure if she's home. She's all over the place right now."

Finding my handbag, I dig out my phone and dial her.

It takes a while, but she finally answers.

"Cassie."

She sounds so happy. I'm about to break her heart.

Should I have let Patrick do this after all?

Tears well in my eyes.

"Lauren."

"Are you okay? Is it Mark? What's happening?"

I swallow hard. Patrick's hand lands on my shoulder and gives it a squeeze.

"I don't want to tell you over the phone, but I need you to decide if you want to see him before …"

Oh God. I'm not doing this well at all.

"Lauren, Mark passed away this afternoon."

"What?" she gasps.

"Patrick says it was a heart attack. He was weak and his body just couldn't take anymore." I pause. "He's still here. The funeral director hasn't been yet. Come over and see him."

She sniffs. "I don't know if I can."

I feel so bad. If she was here, I could hug her and be there for her. She's not far away, but right now it feels like a million miles.

"We're right here if you need us. Come and stay if you want to."

"Isn't Patrick staying with you?"

I close my eyes. "He is, but there's always Sophie's spare bed. I can pull it out and you can sleep on that."

"I'll pack some things and come over."

I hesitate to ask the next question, but I have to—I can't let anything happen to her.

"Lauren, are you okay to drive?"

There's silence for a moment, and I wonder if she's about to lose it at me. She has a very loose relationship with alcohol and although she thinks I don't know, it's been obvious for a while.

"I'm okay. I haven't had anything to drink today."

"Then come over and stay with us. We love you."

"I love you too."

I chew my bottom lip as I end the call. I'm not sure how I'm going to juggle all this grief. Mine and Sophie's will be tough enough, but Lauren's as well? I know she's a grown adult— we're not that far apart in age—but she needs some TLC too.

Patrick grips my shoulder. "She coming over?"

I nod. "Yeah. She'll be here soon."

"You said something about Sophie having a spare bed?"

"There's a pull-out under her bed."

He wraps his arms around my shoulders and kisses my temple. "I'll get that organised when Sophie wakes up."

I meet his gaze. "You don't have to. You've already done so much."

"I'm here to make your life easier. You're not getting rid of me that easy, Cassie Warren."

It's not that I don't appreciate his help—I'm not sure what I'd do without it. But there will come a time when I have to stand on my own, and he won't be around.

So I can't come to depend on him.

I need to do things for myself.

But for just a little while, I'll take the help that's offered.

It's not long before Lauren walks in the front door. She takes one look at Mark on the couch and her lower lip quivers.

I wrap my arms around her, and she holds onto me like her life depends on it.

"Was it quick?" she whispers.

"It didn't take long. They gave him meds for the pain, and he went to sleep."

She lets out a choked sob. "I'm glad it was peaceful."

"He loved you. He loved you so much. Stay with us."

Lauren nods. "Can I sit with him?"

"Of course you can. The funeral director's coming soon, but I'm not sure exactly when. We'll all keep him company."

She sits on the floor beside the couch and takes Mark's hand in hers. "I'm sorry I wasn't here, Mark. I love you. I'm going to miss you so much."

Tears pool in my eyes again. I don't want to intrude on her moment with her brother, but we're all here until he goes.

I drop into a chair nearby, and she gives me a grateful look.

"Thank you for calling me," she says.

"Of course."

"I had this feeling earlier today. Like something crawling over my skin. I thought … I thought it was just me."

I nod. "I understand. It all happened so quick."

Tears roll down her cheeks. "I love him so much."

"I know, honey. I know."

Patrick walks into the room with a tray of coffee cups, Sophie trailing behind with the biscuits.

"I thought you ladies might like something to keep you going while we wait."

Lauren nods. "Thank you."

It's over an hour later that the funeral director arrives. Lauren, Sophie, and I sit in the dining room, out of the way, and hold hands.

Everything happens around me.

I see it. I hear it. But I'm so numb it means nothing.

They carry Mark out and I hold Sophie tight as they close the door behind them, Patrick in tow.

I'm so glad he's here. I don't know if I could do this alone, and Lauren's just as lost as I am.

When it's done, Patrick comes back in.

I meet his gaze. "Everything okay?"

He nods. "They'll call in the morning and we can go over what you need."

"He wanted to be cremated and for us to have a funeral. There's insurance …"

Patrick crosses the room and takes my hand in his, giving it a squeeze. "I'll help you through it."

"I'm glad you're here."

Mark inviting Patrick has turned out to be one of the biggest gifts he could give me because I'm not sure how to do this alone.

Not that I ever wanted to tell him that.

Even in death, Mark's anticipating my needs.

"Me too. I'm so sorry for your loss." He squats in front of the chair. "Anything you need, just tell me. That goes for Lauren and Sophie too. I'll stay as long as I have to."

"Thank you."

"How about I clean up in here and get you three comfortable?"

I nod, but I feel nothing.

I'm aware I have to hold it together for Sophie's sake, and to some extent, Lauren's. It's what Mark would have wanted.

But I have no idea how to do that.

26

CASSIE

The only thing I feel the day of the funeral is empty.

Mark taught me a lot about love. I learned that the human heart has the capacity for so much love; there's space for both him and Patrick. He told me falling in love with him didn't diminish what I felt for the father of my daughter.

I'm not brave enough yet to tell him he's Sophie's father, though.

I know I have to—I'm sure he'll be over the moon. But so much has happened, and I'm reluctant to explode the truce we have going.

It's all a lot to deal with, but for today I'm setting it all aside to mourn the man who's been my partner the past eight years.

A gentle tap on the door wakes me out of my thoughts.

"Come in."

The door opens with a soft click and Patrick steps through. His presence is reassuring—when he's here I can nearly forget the past. We've all been leaning on him heavily, but he's taken it in his stride.

"I don't want to rush you …"

"It's time to go."

He nods. "Sophie and Lauren have headed out to the car. I asked them to give you a minute."

"Thank you." I push myself off the bed and walk toward the door, meeting his gaze.

I'm so confused. After all this time, I never thought Patrick would be a part of my life. But something tells me he's not about to walk away.

Mark told me to move on and be happy, but how can I even consider it when my heart's so broken?

Patrick reaches for me, and I close my eyes as I fall into his arms.

"It's okay, Cassie. We'll get through today together. I'm not going anywhere." He plants a kiss in my hair. "I've got you."

I pull back and nod. "Thank you."

Everything's so easy with him—just as it always was. Guilt tugs at me even though I'm not doing anything wrong.

This is all what Mark wanted.

I have to remember that.

Taking a deep breath, I follow him out to the car. Lauren and Sophie sit in the back and Lauren reaches over and gives my arm a squeeze as I take the front passenger seat.

"We'll be okay, Cassie. Let's celebrate his life."

It's not a far drive, and we walk into the funeral parlour chapel together.

Mark's coffin is already at the front, and the sight of it nearly brings me to my knees.

Patrick slips an arm around me and guides me to the front row of seats.

Lauren and Sophie sit either side of me.

I grimace when Ian walks in, but Lauren slides her hand in mine.

"Ugh why is *he* here?" I sigh.

"I guess because he was Mark's friend."

She rolls her eyes. I stifle a laugh.

"There'll be all kinds of people here today. We just have to get through it."

Lauren leans her head against mine. "You're right."

As the service starts, I hold it together. But when Patrick gets up to speak because he's the only one of us who can, it becomes harder.

"Mark was a simple man—his words, not mine." Patrick smiles. "All he wanted in life was to work with his hands and love his family. I had the huge privilege of becoming friends with him after his diagnosis, and we talked about this day a lot. He didn't want today to be sad. He wanted it to be full of love and laughter. And he wanted the world to know how happy his life was. Eight years ago, Mark met the love of his life, Cassie." He meets my teary gaze. "It was love at first sight, and he said when he met Sophie, that love grew even bigger."

Sophie reaches for my hand and squeezes it tight.

"Nothing made Mark happier than being at home with his girls. That includes his sister, Lauren, who he told me was always a handful."

Lauren laughs softly, and I tighten my grip on her hand.

"He loved you all so much. Mark was also larger than life. I remember the first time he and Cassie welcomed me into their home. He'd had the worst news imaginable, but the first thing he did was offer me a beer and we sat and watched cricket. We didn't have much time, but I'm proud to be able to call him my friend."

The service isn't long—Mark didn't want it to be.

And then we're all in the car and travelling to the crematorium for a private cremation.

It gives me time to gather my thoughts before I face everyone at the wake.

After more brief words from Patrick, Lauren squeezes my hand.

"I love you," she says.

I smile through my tears. "I love you too."

We cling to each other as we make our way to the car.

A moment later, we're travelling to a nearby pub for the wake.

I smile to myself. It's so Mark.

He planned everything out the way he wanted it.

I finally relax.

Lauren, Sophie, and I sit in a corner with drinks and food.

Patrick walks toward us. "You all set, ladies?" he asks.

"Thank you for speaking today when we couldn't," Lauren says.

Patrick leans over, embraces her, and gives her a warm smile. "You're welcome. I know how much you all loved him."

He spends the afternoon hovering as people come and talk to us. He's always attentive and taking care of anything we need.

And then he drives us home.

"Are you staying tonight, Patrick?" Sophie asks.

He ruffles her hair, and she rolls her eyes at him. "I sure am. I thought we could do pizza and watch a movie."

"Yes, please. Mum, is that okay?"

Patrick meets my gaze. I should be angry that he's making plans with her without talking to me first, but I don't have the energy for that today.

"It sounds good. Lauren?"

Lauren shakes her head. "I just want some time to myself. No offence."

"I understand." I give her a quick hug. "But I don't want you to become a stranger. We're sisters."

She nods. "We are. I love you two."

"We love you." I squeeze her forearm. "I'll text you and we'll go for coffee later this week."

"That would be perfect."

I hate to think of her in the house she shared with Mark all alone, but we all have to move on and live our lives.

She gives us a little wave before she makes her way to the front door, and I sigh when she's gone.

"Is she going to be okay?" Patrick asks.

"In time." I rub the back of my neck. "Mark practically raised her. She was only ten when their parents died, and he stepped up."

He runs his fingers through his hair. "Shit. I knew they were close, but …"

"Yeah. I already worry about her for other reasons, but losing Mark is a huge blow."

"I'm sorry. I wish I could do more."

"Lauren was right. We all needed you to speak today. Thank you for being here."

His jaw tightens. "I couldn't be anywhere else."

"And thanks for your pizza suggestion—even if you didn't run it past me first." I raise an eyebrow, and Patrick's lips curl into a smile.

"Yeah. Sorry about that. All I could think about was giving you a break. You must be exhausted."

Why does he have to be so good to me?

I think I'd have preferred it if he'd walked away.

27

PATRICK

Today was one of the toughest days of my life.

Mark had my life—the one I dreamed of. He lived with and loved the woman I loved and raised a girl I suspect might be mine.

Or is that wishful thinking?

I've not asked outright how old Sophie is, but she's a blend of Cassie and me in looks—and we just clicked from day one.

But Mark was also a decent man—a wonderful partner to Cassie and father to Sophie. The world's a much darker place without him in it.

His life being cut short the way it has been is nothing short of cruel.

"I'm glad you're here."

Sophie's voice shakes me out of my thoughts, and I beam a fond smile at the girl. I should be so lucky to have a daughter like her—maybe in time, even if she's not biologically mine, I could win her mother back and have that.

Cassie will need time, but I have plenty of that.

"Me too, kiddo. How are you doing?"

She shrugs. "I'm okay. Sad, but Dad would have loved the attention."

I smile. "You're right. He would have."

"I worry about Mum. She's so sad."

I nod. "She will be. But it'll get better. I promise."

"You should come back for my birthday. It's in September."

I smile. "Three more months, huh?"

"Yeah. Mum's stressing about a group of teenagers in the house, but maybe you could help keep her sane."

I chuckle. "How old will you be?"

"Thirteen." She flicks her ponytail over her shoulder— just like her mother used to do. She's so much like Cassie, but with dark hair and blue eyes.

Could she be mine?

I can't push this—not yet. Cassie's still raw after Mark's death and she will be for some time. But that doesn't stop me from being there for her, and for Sophie. And even if Sophie's not mine, I really like the kid.

Being with them is the easiest thing in the world.

There are still so many questions I want answers to.

But I'm a patient man. It's been fourteen years.

What's another few months?

All I know is that now I'm in their lives, I don't want to let them go.

28

CASSIE

I thought I knew pain when I lost my parents, but Mark's death casts a long shadow.

It's sometimes difficult to get up in the mornings, but Sophie needs me and she gives me strength on the days I have none.

And then there's Patrick.

True to his word, he's a constant in our lives now.

He has to know Sophie's his daughter, but he's not said a word to me. Maybe he's giving me space until I'm ready to acknowledge it.

Lauren comes and goes. She's burying her grief in front of us, but I suspect in private she's drinking.

It's all a lot to cope with.

Patrick's always there—whenever he can get away from work—but he's at pains to keep on the edge of our lives. He never pushes, never tries to bulldoze his way in.

His presence is a source of both worry and comfort.

By the time Sophie's birthday rolls around, I'm not concerned that he's with us for the weekend.

Lauren's here, but I'm grateful for the extra help given that we'll have a house full of teenage girls.

"Hey," he says softly. "I hope you don't mind me intruding on your weekend."

I shake my head. "No. Not at all. I'm not so outnumbered with you and Lauren around."

He chuckles. "Maybe I should get out of here."

"Don't you dare. I need someone to commiserate with."

"Patrick, you're here." Sophie runs across the living room and launches herself into his arms. It's all I can do to hold it together as he hugs her, his eyes closed as if this means as much to him as it does me.

"Where else would I be when it's my favourite girl's birthday?" He lets her go. "I might even have a present here somewhere."

He digs into his bag and pulls out a parcel.

I raise my eyebrows at him, but he just grins.

"Happy birthday, Sophie."

He hands it to her, placing a kiss in her hair.

Tears prick my eyes.

"Thanks, Patrick." She pecks him on the cheek and dives at the couch before ripping her parcel open. "Oh my God. An iPad?"

"Patrick, it's too much." I meet his gaze.

He grips my forearm. "Let me treat her. I want to take care of both of you."

Sophie leaps off the couch and tackles him in a hug. I can't stop smiling—it's so good to see them together.

"Hey, kiddo. I know it's been a tough year. I just wanted

to get you something you'd really enjoy." He fixes his gaze on me. "And maybe you can keep in touch with it? I'll give you my email address. Let me know when you and your mum need anything."

"It's the best. Thank you." She pecks him on the cheek again and heads back to the couch where she starts unboxing it all.

"I should tell you off."

He shrugs. "Maybe, but I know how much you love her and how much she'll benefit from this." Leaning closer, he drops his voice to just above a whisper. "It's not just Sophie I want to keep in touch with. I'm not above sexting with you."

I clap my hand over my mouth and let out a squeak as I suppress a laugh. "Stop it."

"It's good to see you laughing."

"You shouldn't be flirting with me."

"If it brings a smile to your face, I'm going to keep on doing it."

"You can flirt with me if you want." Lauren walks in from the kitchen and shoots him a wink.

Patrick chuckles.

I roll my eyes.

Five thirteen and fourteen-year-old girls for the night— all camped out in the living room. It's going to be a long weekend.

Patrick steals the show.

From the moment they arrive, he's the centre of attention much to Sophie's delight and his obvious discomfort.

The good-looking boy turned into a very handsome man.

"Help," he mouths at me, surrounded by the girls all gushing over Sophie's new iPad.

"Girls, the food is ready. Come and help yourselves."

"Thank you," he murmurs.

"Wouldn't want you getting all that attention." I nudge his ribs with my elbow.

He laughs. "Hey. Once upon a time that might have been right, but they are far too young for me. I'm old enough to be their father."

My throat tightens. "Yeah, I guess you are."

He nudges me back. "Not that you look any older than you did in school."

I bark out a laugh. "Liar."

Leaning closer, he murmurs in my ear, "Still beautiful."

My heart thuds so loud, I barely hear the commotion at the table at first.

Sophie—my beautiful Sophie—has a slice of pizza in her hand.

"All I'm saying is that you don't want to eat too much of that, or you'll end up like your mother." Jessica smirks.

I've always suspected that kid had a mean streak. She hides it well, but the odd comments here and there have added up since Sophie started high school.

What the hell?

Patrick clears his throat.

Jessica's smirk disappears from her face. Her cheeks flush red. She's a ringleader when it comes to these girls and while I shouldn't encourage this, I'm glad Patrick's here.

Jessica just stares at him. Where was this when we were younger? He wasn't witness to any of the bullying I received, but it took him a long time to pull his head out of his arse. And even then …

Sophie covers the distance between them and wraps her

arms around his waist. He gives her a tight hug and kisses the top of her head. "Eat that pizza and don't feel guilty about it," he murmurs.

She giggles, and it makes me smile.

"I hope there's enough pizza for me," Patrick says.

I bite down a grin. He's kept fit—it's obvious. The girls have been obvious in their admiration, and maybe him joining them will encourage them not to worry about a one-off meal for a party.

And even though he said he needed rescuing earlier, he throws himself back into my—our—daughter's party for her.

I'm so confused.

Losing Mark is still so fresh, but Patrick's here and he's real and he seems to want to spend time with us.

Time. I need more time.

———

As the afternoon stretches into evening, I close my eyes as familiar pain hits behind them.

"Are you okay?" Patrick asks.

I pinch the bridge of my nose. "I've got a headache coming on. I get them from time to time."

"Have you seen a doctor about them?"

Biting my bottom lip to stop myself from laughing, I nod. "I was in an accident years ago. They're a lasting reminder of that."

His brows knit. "An accident?"

"That conversation we've been meaning to have …" The pain hits again, and I rub my forehead.

"Hey, let's get you some pain relief, huh? Do you have anything special you take for it?"

I shake my head. "I've got some ibuprofen. Usually that and a sleep helps, but …" I wave my hands in the general direction of the girls.

"They'll be fine. They're in their pyjamas and plenty of movies to watch. There's food and they're all set up for if they ever go to sleep."

I force a smile. "I guess."

"You would have left them in the living room later anyway. They're having fun without us old folks getting in the way."

I laugh softly. "What are you going to do?"

"I'm coming with you to make sure you're okay."

My eyebrows rise. "Patrick, you can't—"

"Let's get this ibuprofen into you, and I'll talk to your daughter to make sure she knows where we are, and then we'll get you to bed."

I would argue, but another burst of pain hits and I know he's right.

My bedroom is cool and quiet, and I close my eyes.

These don't happen often, but the doctor can't find any medical reason for my headaches and they're not common.

But I have been more stressed recently as we planned this party.

It's nothing special. Just some drinks and nibbles while the girls watch some movies and crash here for the night. But with us both feeling Mark's absence, I wanted things to be extra special for Sophie.

Her easy acceptance of Patrick helps.

I strip out of my jeans and T-shirt before tugging off my bra and slipping a stretchy nightgown over my head. I've had it since I moved here and Gran bought me all new clothes, and while it's getting old, it's the most comfortable thing I've got.

A tap on the door makes me look up.

"Come in."

Patrick enters the room and closes the door behind him. He casts his gaze up and down me, and I feel like I'm under the microscope.

I must look a sight in my ratty old nightgown.

"How are you feeling?"

I shrug. "It'll take a while to work. Girls okay?"

He nods. "They're fine. Lauren's got them. I told her I'd be in here."

My eyebrows rise. "Really?"

"You don't think I'm going to leave you to deal with this alone, do you?"

"It's just a headache."

He steps forward until he's right in front of me. "Maybe you can tell me about this accident, so I know what we're dealing with."

My heart thuds.

I wince as the pain twinges, and he grips my shoulder. "Let's get you to bed."

He walks around to the other side of the bed.

"What are you doing?"

"Lying on your bed. It's my job now to make sure you're okay."

I roll my eyes. "And you're going to do that in *my* bed?"

He holds up his palms. "I just want to hold you."

My heart leaps. That does sound good. My bed's been so cold and lonely without Mark, and Patrick's been my rock.

This doesn't help my confusion, but the painkillers are kicking in and I'm drowsy now.

Once my head's down, it won't take long to fall asleep.

I pull back the covers and slip into bed.

Beside me, the bed sinks.

If I wasn't feeling off, I might protest more, but he's taking care of me and for the first time in a while, it's nice to feel pampered.

When I open my eyes, he's lying beside me on top of the blanket, his worried gaze taking me in.

"Tell me about your accident," he murmurs.

I draw in a deep breath. "It was a few weeks after you moved away—the weekend before I was heading to Auckland. We were in the car and Dad was t-boned by a truck driver who went through a red light."

His eyes grow wild and search mine. "What? Were they okay? Is that why they're not here?"

I nod. "They were both killed instantly. I was lucky to survive. But I broke both legs and had a spinal fracture."

"Oh God, Cassie. I had no idea."

"It's not something I like talking about."

"I'm so sorry. Your parents … Mine have no idea that happened. I used to call your house to try and talk to you, but the phone would just ring and ring and then one day the line was disconnected."

"That's when I came to stay here. This was my grandmother's house. She took me in, and we sold our house. After she died, I met Mark and he moved in with us."

He cups my cheek. "I have so many questions for you."

"I'm sure you do, but I've reached my limit tonight. I really need to get some sleep."

Patrick brushes my lips with his. "Okay. I won't push you. Not yet, anyway."

For a moment, I just stare into his eyes. He's being so understanding and while it's sweet, I want him to push me. I want to rage at him for what he did to me back then.

But I can't.

I can't bring myself to do it when he's here for me.

Rolling over, I close my eyes as he makes himself the big spoon.

For just a little while, I can enjoy the warmth of his body behind me.

His hard chest against my back gives me comfort.

His legs tucked behind mine make me feel less alone.

His hand rests lightly on my stomach, and I know I'm safe here with him.

My mind and my heart are still conflicted but in this moment, I'm more at peace than I have been since Mark died.

I know if Sophie needs anything, she's got Patrick.

And just as I thought, it doesn't take long for sleep to pull at me.

I never thought I'd ever fall asleep in Patrick Cross's arms again, but here I am.

———

My headache's gone by the time sun peeks through the small gap in the curtains.

I think back to the last time I woke up with him. At least

this time he's not crowding me in. It's almost like he knows to back off in his sleep.

How the hell did we get here? I never thought I'd ever see him again. And now he's stepping in in the absence of my partner—the man I thought I was spending the rest of my life with.

Guilt weighs heavily on me, especially as we're in the same house where I lived with Mark. And we're lying in the same bed I slept in with Mark.

But Mark would approve of this. When he knew his time was limited, he gave his blessing to us.

I still miss him. At the same time, Patrick has worked his way into my heart again.

One day soon, I'm going to have to front up to the fact that he's Sophie's father. The day that happens, he'll be a part of our lives forever.

That's not a bad thing, but it's a scary thing. I'm not sure what kind of relationship he'll want with me, and I don't know how angry he'll be when I tell him. There's a part of me that's frightened that he will walk away and just want a relationship with Sophie. But there's also a part of me that's frighten that he will want a relationship with me.

I don't want to open my eyes.

Patrick's warmth is still beside me, and I'm so comfortable that the thought of moving isn't fun. I could lie in bed like this forever.

When I do open my eyes, Patrick's propped up on one elbow watching me.

"You know this is the first time we've spent the whole night together. Remember when we fell asleep and you freaked out because we slept until two in the morning?"

I laugh, but then the pain of the party night hits. I should be over it—I thought I was, but Patrick being here brings it all back.

"Mum was waiting in the kitchen. She knew what I'd been up to."

He chuckles. "She knew I'd defiled her daughter?"

That makes me laugh again. He's so good for me, even if I'm struggling sometimes with the past. "Oh, she knew, but she just wanted to make sure I was safe. I don't think she could sleep until I was home." I sigh. "I know what that's like now I'm the mother of a teenager. I'm not sure what I'm going to do when she starts dating."

Patrick rolls onto his back. "That's enough to give *me* nightmares. She's far too sweet to be allowed anywhere near boys."

"I'm so proud of her." I roll to face him.

"We … uhh … we still need to talk."

He knows.

"I know. Just give me time."

He turns toward me, pressing his forehead to mine. "I can do that. You're worth it."

"I hope so," I whisper.

"It's too soon for you. I'm not heartless. And I know how much you loved Mark."

Tears prick my eyes. "I miss him."

"I know you do, baby. I didn't know him long, but I miss him too."

He pulls away and meets my gaze.

"I'm glad you became friends before he died," I say.

"He gave me his blessing, you know?" Patrick reaches out

and tucks a lock of hair behind my ear. "So, I'm going nowhere, Cassie. Not while you need me."

I think I'll always need you.

"That's so him—always thinking of me and Sophie."

"He loved you. And I do too. But I can wait."

Patrick opens his arms to me, and I move closer and into them. He kisses my temple. "I don't want to get out of bed."

"Me either. But I've got a living room full of teen girls who will want breakfast." I place my hand on his hip. "So you'd better get dressed because I'm not sure they can cope with seeing you like this."

He chuckles. "Oh, this look is just for you."

His eyes tell me how he's feeling—but it's too soon for me.

I'm glad he's determined to stick around, but a part of me is terrified that it'll all go wrong again.

I need time to work out how I feel.

29

CASSIE

The first Christmas without Mark is hard.

He and Sophie had their own traditions—they were the ones who insisted on putting up the tree and decorating it.

He's been gone for six months now but Patrick steps in without hesitating, and listening to Sophie laugh as each decoration is hung brings some sunshine back into my life.

Patrick encouraged me to dust off the barbecue and get some actual sun today, and for the first time in a while, I'm completely relaxed.

"What did you tell your parents to explain why you're not with them for Christmas?" I ask.

He chuckles and flips the steaks over. "I told them I was going away. It's not the first year I've taken a break over Christmas and New Year and gone on a trip. They don't need to know I'm only a couple of hours away."

I close my eyes and just enjoy the warmth of the sun

beating down. The store's closed for two weeks, and Sophie's on school holidays so the three of us are spending the time together. I'm still keeping Patrick at arm's length—it's only right. But his company's welcome.

"Is Lauren coming over today?" he asks.

I shrug and open my eyes. "I'm not sure. She has an open invitation, but we don't see her very often."

He nods. "Mark used to worry. I hope she'll be okay."

Scrubbing my face with my hands, I sigh. "Me too. She doesn't have a healthy relationship with herself. I think there's a lot of childhood trauma there, and then losing him …"

"I'm sorry to hear that. If there's anything I can do."

I meet his gaze and shake my head. "I'm not sure there's anything either of us can do, but I appreciate the thought."

Sophie bounces out the back door—she has far too much energy for me. "When's dinner?"

"Very soon. Just finishing off these steaks and I'll put the meat out and we can eat."

She drops into a chair next to me. "Then we can eat the pavlova?"

I spent half the day baking yesterday in preparation for our meal today, and I nod. "Yes, we can have the pav."

Sophie applauds.

I jump when the front door slams and raise my hand to my chest.

"What was that?" Sophie asks.

"I'll go." Patrick's already at the door and heading into the living room.

Giggles float through the air and my heart sinks.

Lauren's unsteady on her feet, and Patrick guides her to a chair before taking a step back.

"Merry Christmas." She throws up her arms to the sky.

"Lauren. It's good to see you."

Her eyes are glazed over, and a pit forms in the base of my stomach.

"It's good to see you too," she slurs, and tears prick my eyes.

"How did you get here?" Patrick asks.

"Taxi."

I breathe a sigh of relief. Now she's in my home, I'm not letting her leave.

"We're about to have dinner. There's plenty of food."

She nods. "Food would probably be a good idea."

I exchange a glance with Patrick.

"It's the first Christmas without him."

I place my hand over hers. "I know it's tough, Lauren."

She nods. "I don't have anyone."

"That's not true. You have me and Sophie. We love you."

Tears well in her eyes. "I miss him so much."

"So do we."

I close my eyes when Sophie speaks. She shouldn't see this, but Lauren needs to know we're here for her.

Patrick places plates of meat on the table. "I hope you guys are hungry." He sits on the other side of me and reaches under the table, giving my knee a reassuring squeeze.

It's nice to be taken care of—it's something I don't want to get used to in case it disappears overnight, but while keeping an eye on Lauren, I eat.

The more she eats, the more she seems to sober up.

"I haven't had barbecue in forever," she moans. "This is so good."

"I'm glad you're enjoying it." Patrick smiles at me, and I force a smile back.

After dinner and dessert, Lauren leans back and pats her stomach. "I needed that."

Sophie and Lauren chat as the sun sets, and when the sky grows dark, I've had enough of sitting around.

I clap my hands together. "Why don't we go inside and have some coffee?"

Lauren follows me inside, and I pause as we enter the living room.

"Stay here the night. You can sleep in the spare room."

She shakes her head. "No, I don't want to interfere."

"You're not. It's Christmas and you're family."

Her eyelashes flutter as she shifts her gaze to Patrick. "And Doctor Dreamy?"

"Let me take care of that."

She nods. "I'm not sure how much longer I can stand."

As if on queue, she slumps and Patrick catches her before she falls. He scoops her up bridal style and looks at me. "Spare room?"

Lauren runs her red-painted fingernails down his cheek. "You're gorgeous. Cassie needs her head read if she hasn't just snapped you up yet."

"Is that right?" Patrick's bemused tone tells me he at least isn't taking her seriously. My burning cheeks say otherwise.

"If she doesn't want you—I'm available." She cackles, and Patrick carries her up the hallway and into the spare room. I rush ahead and turn down the sheet so he can place her on the bed.

He backs away, and I step forward again to pull the blanket over her.

"You're such a good mother, Cassie. Maybe you could be my mum." Lauren laughs.

"Maybe just for tonight. Get some sleep."

I pause in the doorway. It only takes moments for soft snores to fill the air.

My heart aches for her, and I'm not sure I can do anything to help that.

When I walk into the living room, Patrick's waiting on the couch with two coffee mugs on the table. "How is she?"

"Asleep already."

He chuckles and picks up his mug. "I'm not surprised."

"I'm so worried about her."

He takes a sip of his drink, seeming to mull over his reply. "I can tell. She's really not handling this well, is she? Maybe I can make some enquiries about getting her help."

I sigh. "That would be good. But I think she also needs to want to help herself."

"That's the tough part." He puts his mug on the coffee table and turns to face me. "Sophie's in her room. So, now I've got you alone, there's something I need to do."

"What's that?"

He leans over and kisses me softly on the lips.

My heart thuds.

"Merry Christmas, Cassie." He runs his fingers through my hair. "I've got something for you."

"You didn't have to. I don't have anything for you."

Patrick smiles. "Are you kidding? I get to spend time with my girls."

My throat tightens. It's too soon. I can't …

"I know this must be hard." He continues, "First Christmas without Mark. So I wanted to make things special because he would have wanted you to be spoiled rotten."

I laugh softly. "I'm pretty sure you're using that as an excuse."

"Maybe. But it's also true."

He picks up something from the couch beside him and passes it to me. It's a long black box, tied up with a ribbon and almost too pretty to open.

"Open it," he says as if reading my mind.

I tug at the ribbon and it falls away before I lift the lid of the box.

Inside is a long silver chain and a pedant in the shape of an infinity symbol. The stones in the pendant sparkle in the light.

"It's beautiful," I croak.

He plucks it out of the box, and I turn around and lift my hair out of the way so he can put it on me. When it's clipped together, he rests his hands on my shoulders and I close my eyes when he leans in and places a kiss on the nape of my neck.

"This is my commitment to you," he whispers. "For what we had before, what we have now, and what we'll have in the future—if you let me in."

"I want to let you in, but it's too soon."

He nods. "I know it is. That's why I'm giving you this now so you know I'll be waiting when you're ready."

I reach for it, placing my hand on it and feeling the roughness of the stones. It's a little overwhelming—I'm not used to getting jewellery. Mark was more practical and less romantic when it came to gift giving.

There was no doubt in my mind that he loved me, but he wasn't very good at expressing himself.

"Do you want to sleep in my bed tonight?" I hold my palm out. "Just like the night of Sophie's party. Not anything more than that."

He looks sheepish. "I'm glad you asked. I'm not sure my back could survive a night on your couch."

"I think I might get off to bed and have an early night. Thank you so much for the pendant. It's beautiful."

Patrick smiles. "I just wanted to make it clear how much you mean to me. I'm well aware that we have a lot to talk about and resolve before we move forward. And I know you need time. But I've got you."

I rise from the couch. "I appreciate it."

"I'll make sure we're all locked up and follow you."

By the time I reach the bedroom, my heart's pounding in my ears.

But after changing and slipping into bed, I'm out as soon as my head hits the pillow.

———

Lauren's standing in the kitchen when I walk out.

She turns as I enter the room, one hand on the jug, the other on a coffee mug. "I'll grab another cup," she says.

"That would be good."

"Can we talk?"

"Of course we can." I give her hip a squeeze.

"Go and sit in the living room and I'll bring in the coffee."

I sit in the silence for a few moments before she walks in

with two mugs that she places on the coffee table before taking a seat on the couch next to me.

"I wanted to apologise for yesterday. I'm so sorry."

I shake my head. "It's okay. You were safe under my roof last night, and that's all that matters."

Tears well in her eyes. "I'm making such a mess of things. Mark would be so angry."

"Mark would understand." I reach for her hand. "He loved you so much, Lauren, and he didn't want to leave you any more than he wanted to leave me."

"The things I said, though. I hit on Patrick right in front of you …"

"But you wouldn't do it sober. I know that."

"I just want what you have." She sniffs. "I just want someone who'll be there for me and love me. You got two of them."

"I'm greedy." I risk a small smile, and she lets out a snort. "Drinking isn't the answer, though."

"I know." She tilts her head as she looks at me. "I promise I'll try and do better."

"The last thing I want to do is lose you too."

She bites her bottom lip. "So, Patrick slept with you last night?"

"He slept in my bed, yes." I lower my head and look at her thought my eyelashes. "*Someone* was in the spare bed."

Lauren studies me closely. "Are you two …?"

"No. He's been the perfect gentleman." I swallow hard. "I don't want you to think I'm moving on yet."

Her eyes widen. "I wouldn't judge you if you did. Mark wanted you to be happy, and I know he approved of Patrick."

"It's only been six months."

She squeezes my hand. "You have to grab love when it's right there, Cassie." Her eyes drop to my neck. "What's that?"

Letting go of my hand, she reaches for my pendant.

"Patrick gave it to me for Christmas."

She smiles. "You have my blessing too when you're ready."

"That means a lot."

The fall of footsteps makes us both look up. Patrick stands in the doorway, glancing between us. "Have you two had breakfast?"

I shake my head. "No, just coffee."

"How about I cook up the leftover bacon and some eggs? There are some English muffins in the pantry."

"Oh, that sounds amazing." Lauren claps her hands together.

"Perfect for a hangover." He shoots a wink at her, and she sighs.

He heads into the kitchen, and she leans over. "He looks that good first thing in the morning, and he cooks breakfast. That's a keeper if you ask me."

She laughs, and for a moment I see the real her—the one who's not hiding behind the alcohol.

It's a sight I wish we saw more often.

30

PATRICK

Nine months later

Yesterday, my daughter turned fourteen.

There are no doubts in my mind—she's mine. Even if I'm not her biological father, she turns to me for everything she would have gone to Mark for.

I'm not sure if Cassie knows just how much Sophie and I talk to each other—giving her the iPad opened up her world to me.

But Cassie trusts me, and I'd do anything to retain that trust to the point that I still haven't asked her flat out if Sophie's mine.

We still haven't had the conversation we need to.

Am I a coward? Maybe. I don't want to hear about her love story with Mark, but that's a part of her history now. I have questions, but I'm not sure if she'll give me straight answers.

I'm in far too deep to let go. I think I was from the start.

This year I missed Sophie's special day—not because I wanted to but because I had a big surgery. But I'm here the day after and able to spend the whole weekend.

I pull up outside the house and rub my neck.

A car I don't recognise is parked in the driveway.

But I do recognise the man standing on the front doorstep.

Lauren pointed him out at the wake—he's an old friend of Mark's—Ian, and I assume that's the only reason Mark kept him around after he got together with Cassie.

Neither Lauren nor Cassie like him.

"I just wanted to say hello." I hear as I grab my bag and walk up the path.

"I'm not up for visitors. Sorry." Cassie tries to close the door, but he puts his foot in it to stop her.

"Everything okay, Cass?" I ask.

Ian turns and scowls at me.

"Ian was just leaving."

I really hate this guy.

Mark's wake was a long time ago, and I'm not worried about making a scene anymore. Cassie's just way too polite.

"What are you doing here?" he asks.

"Not that it's any of your business, but I'm spending the weekend." Fuck tiptoeing around him just because he was Mark's friend. I'm about to piss a circle around my girls.

My girls.

The thought of that makes my heart swell.

"You don't need to be here anymore. They don't need you. I'm telling you to back off."

I laugh. "Are you kidding me?"

He pulls his foot out the door and turns to face me. I love this. I've got about a foot of height on him and more muscle. I'm not a man who sets out to intimidate others, but I'd do it for free with this guy.

"Mark wouldn't have wanted you sniffing around Cassie and her kid."

"But he would have wanted you?" I raise an eyebrow. "Let me spell this out for you. I've known Cassie since we were five years old, and I have loved her for most of my life. You might have been friends with Mark, but he gave me his blessing before he died."

The colour drains from his face. "He … he did not."

I stab at his chest with my index finger. "He did. And I intend on being here for both Cassie and Sophie. They. Are. Mine."

He shakes his head. "No, you're lying."

"You can believe whatever you want to, but I'm going nowhere. I'll change jobs if I have to."

I'm sure Hamilton hospital wouldn't say no to a surgeon with my skills.

Cassie's closed the door while all this is going on, and I don't blame her. She hates confrontation—always did.

His nostrils flare, but he thinks better of continuing the conversation and storms off toward his car.

I turn back and reach for the front door handle, turning it and stepping into the living room.

"Patrick." Sophie runs and then launches herself into my arms—the standard greeting.

"Hey, princess. Where's your mother?"

"She went out the back to water the garden. I think she wanted to get away from Ian, and you were dealing with him."

"Does he come here often?"

She shakes her head. "He's been here a couple of times, but Mum won't let him in. He's not very good with the word no."

My jaw sets. "Well, I laid down the law. I hope he listens."

"Patrick," she whispers.

"Yes, sweetheart?"

"Are you my dad?"

I swallow hard. All this time, the thought has lingered in the back of my head, but I don't want to voice it so plainly—not yet.

And the last thing I want is for Cassie to think I'm undermining her. "I don't honestly know, Sophie. I hope so."

"Me too." She smiles, and I'm sure I see myself in that smile. "You haven't asked Mum?"

"I didn't want to put more pressure on her. When we met again, she was dealing with Mark's illness and I think she's had enough on her plate this past year, don't you?"

She nods. "It's not as bad as it was. When Dad first died, she'd cry when you weren't here. I think she was trying to be brave for all of us."

"Doesn't she do that anymore?"

"Not very often. I think your visits do her good."

I smile. "I hope so."

"I like it when you visit. Especially on my birthday."

Barking out a laugh, I hold up my bag. "Your present is in here, birthday girl. Let me get inside."

"Come on, then." She grabs my hand and pulls me into the house.

Cassie walks in the door and smiles. "Did you get pounced on?"

I laugh. "Looks like it."

After placing my bag on the other end of the couch, I open it and pull out a parcel. "I'm not sure if this is it or not …"

Sophie's eyes light up. "That's mine."

"Is it?"

"You said it was." She laughs.

"Did I?" I grin.

Cassie rolls her eyes. "You two …"

"Happy Birthday, Sophie." I hand her the parcel, and she kisses me on the cheek.

I grab Cassie's hand as she passes and pull her onto the couch with me. Her green eyes flash with amusement.

"I am going to smack you if it's something expensive." She laughs.

"Yes, please." I grin, and she shakes her head.

Sophie has a laptop for school, but it's getting older and slower. She squeals when she pulls a new one out of the box.

"Patrick." Cassie playfully slaps my arm.

"Let me spoil her."

She nods and looks away.

"Thank you, thank you, thank you." Sophie stands and rushes over, kissing me on the cheek again. "I'm going to go and get it set up."

"Happy birthday," I call out as she races up the hallway.

Cassie sighs. "I don't know what to do about you."

"Anything you want." I've given up holding back. I want

Cassie. Whatever happened in the past is behind us, and we've been rebuilding a new foundation—whether she realises it or not.

She ignores me. "What happened with Ian? Did he give you a hard time?"

I shrug. "Did Mark put up with his bullshit?"

She laughs. "I guess the answer to my question is yes."

I fist my hands and then relax them. "He told me to back off, but I'm not doing that—I can't."

Her expression softens. "Patrick."

"I know you might not be ready, but I am."

Cassie's brow furrows. "Ready?"

"For this. For us."

She blinks rapidly. "I—"

"I love you. I'm not sure I ever stopped. Having you back in my life has been the best thing to happen to me in years. I hate that you had to lose Mark, but I'm right here."

Cassie raises her palm to my chest. Her eyes search mine. "I … I …"

"It's okay to feel again. You know that, right?"

She nods. "It's so hard."

"I know, sweetheart, and I'd give anything to be able to take that pain away. But I want you to know that when you are ready, I'm in it for the long haul."

Tears well in her eyes. "I want to. But I'm so scared. I remember what it was like last time you broke my heart."

"I broke *your* heart? You shut me out."

"You cheated on me." She sniffed.

"No, I didn't."

"I saw you in bed with Vicki."

"When?"

"The night of the party."

I search her eyes for some sign that she's making this up. All I see is hurt—hurt that she's lived with for years.

"There's no way. I didn't …"

"I *saw* you. You said my name when you saw me."

I shake my head. I've got no memory of that. People started arriving, and I'd had one beer. By the time the party was in full swing, I felt tired—really tired. And it was weird because I swore I saw Vicki, but she wasn't invited.

I thought the days before when we were packing had caught up on me.

Did something happen?

If it did, it wasn't anything I consented to.

"I swear, Cassie. I don't remember anything other than being really tired that night. When I woke up in the morning, the house was empty and then I got busy cleaning up because Mum and Dad were on their way back."

"But I …"

"I didn't cheat. Not that I can remember. And that scares the shit out of me because if I can't remember, what happened?"

Tears fall onto her cheeks, and I swipe them away.

"I loved you so much back then. I'd wasted so much time and then lost you all over again. When you didn't turn up at uni, I thought maybe you'd transferred to Otago. It was the toughest year of my life—and I tried to reach you, I really did."

She sniffs. "If you'd told me that back then, I'm not sure I'd have believed you."

"What about now?"

Cassie shrugs. "I don't know what to think."

She closes her eyes and the way her brows knit—is she getting one of her headaches?

"Are you okay?"

Her eyes open and she fixes her gaze on me. "What happened to us, Patrick? How did we lose all those years?"

I move closer. "We were teenagers. Dumb shit happens. But I don't know why you gave me the cold shoulder the way you did. Or why you never told me I have a daughter."

Her eyes. I could live to be a hundred and never forget the devastation in them.

I put it there, but I want the rest of her story.

It's the least I deserve.

31

CASSIE

I feel sick.

All this time and Patrick's either a really good actor or Vicki set the whole thing up.

Why didn't I let him talk to me?

From the moment he asked me out, I was so sure he was going to hurt me that when he did, it wasn't really a surprise.

But he didn't do it?

My head swims.

He grips my elbow. "Put your head between your knees."

I lean over. For years, that night has haunted me. Finding my boyfriend cheating on me a short time after losing my virginity to him hurt so deep that the memory always hit hard—especially when I had Sophie every day to remind me.

"We need to talk about this."

I nod. "I know. Just give me a minute."

Patrick slips his arm around my shoulders.

"I guess communication's never been a strength of ours."

He plants a kiss in my hair, but it doesn't take away the numbness. "We've been so focused on the now that we keep on putting off talking about it. You must know I still have a lot of questions."

I take a deep breath and sit up. "I'm sure you do. You were my first real boyfriend. I was a teenage girl and my heart was broken."

He raises his hand to my cheek. "You broke my heart when you shut me out."

Tears roll down my face. "We're such a mess, aren't we? I keep thinking about what my life—our life would have been if we'd talked."

He takes a sip of his drink. "I ran out of time. Mum and Dad practically had to drag me away when we moved. And when I couldn't get in touch, I knew I had to move on."

"If we hadn't had the accident. If I'd let you in. I feel like my head is full of ifs."

Patrick leans back in his seat, cradling his glass in his hand. "I get it. But I think if we dwell on the ifs, that'll drive us insane."

"I owe you a huge apology."

He shakes his head, leaning forward again and placing his drink on the table. "I owe you one. That party was such a dumb idea in the first place. I didn't care about saying goodbye to all those people—not really. I went along with it because we'd spent so long talking about it before school even ended."

"How do we even start to move forward?"

Patrick reaches for my hand. "You were all that mattered back then. I was so angry with myself for wasting my high school years not being with you, and then I somehow managed to throw away so many more. I'm not even sure after all this time that I can get to the bottom of whatever happened, but I promise you, Cassie—I *never* cheated on you."

My eyes fly open, and our gazes lock. His eyes—so much like our daughter's—are fixed on me.

"Sophie *is* yours. I never planned to keep her from you—I came looking for you once."

His brows rise. "When?"

"Not long after she was born. My pregnancy was tough. I found out about it when I was in hospital after the accident. I knew I had options but I wanted her, and Gran was behind me the whole way."

He squeezes my fingers. "You said you had multiple surgeries."

I nod. "I did. And there were medications they wanted to give me but couldn't because I was pregnant. We worked through it, but I was lucky I had a high pain tolerance because there were times …" Tears prick my eyes. "Giving birth was the easy part. But I was so hormonal and miserable, still dealing with the death of my parents."

"And you came looking for me."

"I found you. You were walking down the road from uni, and you were with another woman. Seeing you hurt me so much—it took me back to the party. So I turned around and came home."

He lets out a sigh. "I think I saw you. There was one day … but I wasn't fast enough and then the car was gone, and I thought maybe it was just wishful thinking."

Pulling away from him, I bury my face in my hands. So many moments—lost opportunities.

"Cassie. Come here." He tugs me into his arms.

"I wanted to tell you about Sophie. But I thought you'd moved on."

"I've seen pregnancy hormones in action. I know they mess you up. But you could have contacted me at any time. It's been years."

My heart sinks. "I know. The longer it got, the harder it got. I thought about it a lot over the years, but I knew I'd left it too long and Mark was so good with her. I'm not sure any excuse is enough."

Patrick places a kiss in my hair. "You asked how we move forward? We tell Sophie the truth."

My throat tightens. "I know you want to, but—"

"No buts. That kid of ours is smart. She's beautiful and funny and kind, and she'll understand."

"I know. It's so hard to think of her growing up. She was a baby five minutes ago."

"I wish I'd seen that."

I raise my fist to my mouth and bite down a sob.

Patrick takes hold of my hand and gives it a gentle rub. "Don't. Please. I know I've missed out, but I'm so in love with you, Cassie Warren. I want us to build a life." He pauses. "You, me, and Sophie. Together."

I meet his gaze. There's so much love in his eyes that I just want to cry. "I'd like that. I'm not sure how, but I'd like that."

"We start with telling our daughter the truth."

Nodding, I swipe the tears from my cheeks with my index finger. "That sounds like a good place to start to me."

He grasps my chin and raises my face to his.

Dropping his hand, he leans closer. My heart pounds so hard, blood rushes in my ears.

He starts soft, his lips caressing mine before I open up and he takes advantage of the situation. His kiss is warm and slow—we haven't been together for so long, but the taste of his lips is familiar—comforting.

The kiss deepens, and I'm swept away in emotion.

I love this man.

I want this man.

Fate brought us back together, and I'm never letting him go again.

When the kiss ends, my cheeks burn with excitement.

And I already know what my future brings.

Patrick's lips twitch. "Was that okay?"

"You know it was more than okay."

"I hoped it was. I'm a bit rusty."

I roll my eyes. "Liar. I know you've had girlfriends."

"Not for a long time. And I've not seen anyone else since the day I first ran into you at the hospital. I knew then what I wanted, and that's never going to change."

"Patrick."

I pull away from him as Sophie's voice comes from the hall doorway.

Her gaze flicks between us, and the smile falls from her face.

"Hey, Soph." Patrick doesn't drop his arm from around me, and I swallow hard.

"What's going on? Mum?"

"I …" I swallow hard. "We were just taking about the past. But there is something we need to tell you."

Sophie glances between us. "What is it?" she asks.

Patrick looks at me before taking my hand in his, giving it a squeeze.

"Patrick's your father."

Tears well in her eyes. "He is?"

I nod. "It's a long story and I don't have all the energy to tell you it today, but he's your real dad."

She smirks. "I'd actually already worked that one out. Duh."

Patrick chuckles. "I knew you were a smart cookie."

She moves closer, dropping to her knees in front of us. "I've got your eyes."

He taps her on the nose. "That was the first thing I noticed."

She bites her bottom lip. "I never really asked Mum about you. I thought you didn't want me."

My eyes fill with tears. We never talked about it because she didn't ask and I never knew how to bring it up. And then Mark came into our lives and took on the stepfather role so completely.

"That was never the case, sweetheart. But I'm glad you had Mark."

Sophie flicks her gaze between us. "You don't mind that I called him Dad, do you?"

Patrick shakes his head. "No. He was your dad for a while. I'm here now."

"Are we moving to live with you?"

He shifts his gaze to me. "We haven't decided anything yet. I think we need some time to adjust to all of this and get used to each other."

I bite down a laugh. I'm sure if Patrick had his way, we'd

be moved in with him already and getting on with our lives. But the reality is far from simple.

Sophie and I have a home here—I have work and she has school. Patrick is in a one-bedroom apartment.

We do need time together both as a couple to make sure we're going to work, and as a family. If things didn't last between Patrick and I, we'd have to work out custody and the thought of that is enough to give me another headache.

The solution in my mind is for us to move to Auckland and get a place for the three of us. It would mean giving up my job here, but there are more jobs up there and I could rent out this place for income.

"So, if you two are together, does that mean I'm finally gonna get a baby brother or sister?" Sophie grins.

I raise my eyebrows.

"Maybe," Patrick says.

I swallow hard. He doesn't know that Mark and I tried to have a baby.

It's bittersweet in some ways, as if we'd had a baby there would've been something left of him.

"Mum?"

I shift my gaze to Sophie. "Yes?"

"Are you okay? You look like you're coming down with one of your headaches."

I reach for her hand. "I'm fine. It's all a lot to take in. I wasn't sure how you would take the news about Patrick. Turns out you're way too smart and it's not a problem. I'm so proud of you."

And just like that, everything's out in the open.

I'm not sure what the future holds, but it looks like we're all facing it together.

32

CASSIE

Spending our first day together as a family is wonderful. Patrick bounces between Sophie and me, and the past months that we've spent together have really helped us build something out of nothing.

He's been in my bed before, but tonight will be different. It's been platonic up until now, but just the thought of the way things changed today leave my heart racing.

What will it be like to be with Patrick now?

I'm about to find out.

Sophie's been in bed a while, and we're crashed out on the couch watching a movie.

Patrick slips his arm around my waist. "I think it's bedtime," he says, then brushes his lips behind my ear.

Standing, he holds his hand out for me to take. The house is locked—he's already checked all of that—and I grab the remote and turn the television off before taking his outstretched hand.

This is it.

"We don't have to do this," he murmurs. "If you want to wait, that's fine. It's enough that we're giving this a go."

"I want to."

And that's the truth. I miss sex. It's just not the act of it, but the intimacy and the companionship that go with it.

The companionship with Patrick is easy. It's been easy since he started coming here. Over the last year and a bit, we've had an opportunity to re-establish the friendship that we enjoyed before we started going out the last time.

He knows the difference between teenage Cassie and adult Cassie as far as my likes and dislikes go. He knows my taste in music, movies, TV, and books.

We've had time to learn about each other.

This relationship will be different from before.

He cups my face in his hands and presses a gentle kiss to my lips.

"Come on."

I tremble in anticipation of what's to come. It's crazy— I'm a grown woman.

When we reach the bedroom, Patrick closes the door quietly behind us. "You're scared."

I nod. "Do you remember the night we were together? I feel like that."

"You don't have to be nervous with me."

"Are you kidding? When you look—"

His brows knit. "Don't you dare finish that sentence. We went through this back then, and I'm telling you now. You. Are. Gorgeous. I want you so fucking much, Cassie."

"But—"

"I get that we're older, but everything gets better with age."

"Or mouldy." I try hard not to laugh, but he's so serious and I can't let this be like that. I want to be able to relax and maybe laughing will help.

"Cassie Warren. I will put you over my knee if you make any more self-deprecating jokes. Do you think I'd have been here every weekend following you around like a puppy needing attention if I didn't want you?"

I swallow hard. Is that what he's been doing?

"I thought you were fulfilling some promise you'd made Mark."

"I was. But I'm also selfish, and I wanted every single second I could get with you." He sits on the end of the bed. "That first day at the hospital. I could barely believe my eyes. I thought I'd gotten over you and moved on, but seeing you again? We had so much unfinished business."

I take a seat beside him. "That's what Mark said to me. That we had unfinished business. I knew it was true—just didn't want to face it."

"And now?"

"There are definitely things I wished I knew more about —like how you ended up in bed with Vicki. If what you say is true, then the truth about how you got there is unimaginable."

His eyes search mine. "You know I'm telling the truth, right?"

"Patrick, it was nearly fifteen years ago. Why would you be lying now? If you didn't want to be in our lives, then you would have disappeared once Mark died."

He slips his arm around my waist. "I never wanted to let you go. Not then, and definitely not now."

We sit there for a moment, before he grasps my chin and pulls my gaze to his. "Our new beginning starts tonight. Are you going to let me show you how much I want you?"

He kisses me, soft at first, but takes my breath away as he builds the kiss's intensity. I'm so lost in this man, the one who broke my heart so long ago but now cradles it as if it's the most precious thing in the world.

"Yes. Yes. I want this. A million times yes," I whisper.

He stands and removes his shirt. It's like all those years ago, but even better.

"I love the way you look at me," he says.

"I love touching you."

"Then do it."

I let my hands trace his abs, pressing my palms to them as I rise to my feet.

"Your turn." His lust-filled eyes give me the strength to do what I did all those years ago. And when I'm standing topless in front of him, he cups my heavy breasts and runs his thumbs over my nipples.

"I'm getting a sense of déjà vu." I laugh.

"Is that so bad?"

"Show me what you've got, Patrick Cross."

He nods toward the bed. "Get on there."

Patrick pounces on me the second I'm on my back on the bed, pinning my arms above my head and unleashing his tongue on my nipples. The years have only made them more sensitive, and I close my eyes and moan at the sensation.

"You're so responsive. I mean, you were before, but this is a whole other level."

"That's what pregnancy did to me."

He chuckles. "If that's the case, then I am getting you pregnant as soon as possible."

"Don't I get a say in that?" I laugh, but when it does happen, it'll be wonderful. I've been clucky the past couple of years, and the thought of Sophie having a sibling makes me so happy.

"Of course. I want to make more babies with you, Cassie. I've never wanted that with anyone else."

"Why me?"

"Because we already made one perfect one. There are more in our future even if they're a bit delayed."

I laugh as he accidentally tickles me, pulling down my skirt. My panties follow, and my heart rate accelerates as he runs his hungry gaze over me.

"So beautiful."

"Show me." I point at his pants, and he grins.

He sheds his jeans and underwear and kneels on the bed.

I lick my lips. "Come here?"

He crawls around the side of me, while I prop myself up on my pillows.

I meet his curious gaze before I grasp his cock at the base and take it in my mouth.

"Oh, Jesus, Cassie. That's …"

He grips the sheet tightly as I suck lightly, sliding my tongue up and down his length. I was way too scared to do this at eighteen, but I'm confident I've got this now. And from the noises he's making, I'm not wrong.

"It's too much, babe. It's been a while, and I don't want to come yet."

I lift my mouth off him with a pop. "Why not?"

He chuckles and lies beside me, tracing circles on my stomach with his fingers.

"Because there's no rush. We have all the time to enjoy each other." He slides his hand down between my legs. "I've thought about our first time so many times."

His gentle touch leaves me breathless as he inserts his fingers into me and then slides them over my clit.

"Me too."

"I loved that we were each other's first."

He repeats the action again and again before pushing on my thigh. I part my legs and he moves between them.

There's no hesitation this time. He bows his head and his tongue works overtime as I arch my back and moan. Patrick pulls me to the brink and then kisses his way over my belly and up to my breasts.

"Patrick," I whine.

"Patience." He grins.

I'm torn between slapping and kissing that grin from his face. "It's not fair."

"Life's not fair." He makes his way down again before plundering my pussy with his mouth, his fingers working overtime pumping in and out of me.

The confidence that wasn't there all those years ago is in abundance, and I'm suddenly jealous of anyone else he was ever with.

This should have always been mine.

And then he takes me over the edge. My pussy clenches down on his fingers, and he lets out a loud breath.

"I need to be inside you."

"I need you inside."

"Do I need a condom?"

I meet his gaze and shake my head. "I'm on the pill."

"Thank God."

He doesn't hesitate. Lining himself up, he pushes into me and pumps a few times before flipping onto his back. "Come here. I need you to ride me."

In the past I would have made some kind of disparaging remark about myself, but Patrick wants me—I can see it in his eyes. I straddle his hips and lower myself onto his hard cock.

"Oh, fuck. Cassie, that feels so good."

He rises with me as I rock against him, his hands covering my breasts, his thumbs rubbing my nipples. When he drops one hand and slips it between us, finding my clit, I gasp.

"That's it. Come with me," he says.

We pick up the pace as his fingers work me over. It doesn't take long for the tension to build—I think we're both on a knife's edge as it is.

I detonate, closing my eyes, my whole body trembling.

He grabs my hips and pulls me down hard as he shouts out a moan.

And then we're both panting as I roll off him, kissing, touching, just enjoying being naked together.

"I'm sorry that didn't last longer. I just wanted you so much."

"I seem to remember telling you that all we needed was practice."

Patrick kisses me hard, cupping my cheek. "This time we get to do this more than once."

"And no parents waiting up for us."

He laughs. "No, we're the parents now. How freaky is that?"

"Very."

———

DESPITE WEARING EACH OTHER OUT, neither of us can sleep.

I'm lying with my back to him, and I close my eyes as he traces the scars on my back.

"I could make these go away, you know?"

His words make me smile.

"I'm sure you could. But I'm done with any surgery, and they don't hurt. They're a reminder what happened, and I don't ever want to forget. The accident changed me—it forced me to grow up."

He places gentle kisses down my spine. "I understand."

"I'm so glad we ran into you at the hospital that day."

Patrick tugs at my arm so I roll onto my back. He props himself up on his elbow to look at me.

"Me too. I never forgot you. There were times when I thought about searching, but I didn't think you'd want me."

I sigh. "I'm still not sure I would have let you explain."

"Doesn't matter now. We're together. How many babies do you want to have?"

I burst into laughter. "Slow down. We only decided to get back together today."

"It's been a while in *my* head." He kisses my temple. "I was just waiting for you to catch up."

"Don't get too far ahead of me."

He drops down onto the bed and slides an arm over me.

"I'll try not to. But I am going to start looking at houses for us."

"Patrick," I growl.

"We'll need to go and see my parents too. There's a lot to catch them up on."

I raise my hands to my face. "Your mother is going to hate me."

"No. She'll be fine. She might be a bit angry at first and then we'll introduce her to her granddaughter. That kid's enough to brighten anyone's day. Let alone her newly discovered grandparents'."

I smile, but the thought terrifies me. All Jane Cross knows is that I broke her son's heart.

I'm not sure how I'm going to face her.

———

For the whole weekend, the three of us are holed up together in the house just being together.

It's bliss.

No one else knows we're together or our story—I have yet to tell Lauren that Sophie is Patrick's. I'm not sure how well that's going to go down when I've kept it from her all that time.

But we've put the past behind us and we're only looking forward.

It's still hard when Patrick has to leave on Sunday to go home.

"See you on Friday, Dad." Sophie's taken to this whole thing like a duck to water. I think it's because she's had it worked out for a while.

Patrick's Adam's apple bobs. She's gone straight for the kill calling him dad, and it's a lot for him to handle.

She hugs him tight and gives him a kiss on the cheek.

"I love you, Sophie. Be good for your mother."

"Love you too."

She glances between us and makes her way back into the house.

"She's amazing," he says.

"I know. We did good."

He pulls me into his arms.

"I don't want to go, but I have to," he murmurs. "You know that, don't you?"

"I do."

"I love you."

I freeze. It's not the first time he's said it, but saying it back to him is hard. But in typical Patrick fashion, he anticipates the reason for my hesitation.

"You'll say it when you're ready." He hugs me tight and kisses my temple. "I know that."

"I'm going to miss you."

"I'll miss you." He leans back and his eyes drink me in. "Being with you again is everything."

"For me too."

I close my eyes as he kisses my forehead. "You call me if that Ian comes around again."

"What are you going to do? Get in the car, drive all the way here, and deal with him?"

"If I have to." He gives my forearms a squeeze. "I'll do whatever it takes to protect my family. See you on Friday."

I wrap my arms around myself when he drives away. And I stay on the driveway until he disappears into the distance.

I'm scared, but I'm in love with Patrick Cross all over again.

Sophie's waiting inside when I walk in the door.

"Are we moving to Auckland?"

I raise my eyebrows. "We just had a whole weekend talking about everything, and now you're asking?"

She shrugs. "You never said we definitely were. I didn't want to ask in front of Dad in case you didn't agree."

I take a step toward her. "What do you want?"

She chews the inside of her cheek for a moment. "I want us to all be together. I love this house, but Dad died here. It makes me sad."

I nod. "That's how I feel. You know Patrick would move in with us if we wanted him to, though?"

"Maybe. But I think I'd like to try living in Auckland."

Smiling, I cover the distance between us and tuck a lock of hair behind her ear. "I think I'd like to try too."

"So let's do it." She beams that beautiful smile at me.

"Okay."

33

CASSIE

Patrick's looking at houses this weekend.

He's over the moon that Sophie and I have agreed to move to be with him.

His apartment isn't big enough for the three of us, but when he asked me if I wanted to join him, I told him I had to work.

Mr Smedley was delighted when I told him what I was up to.

I thought he'd be sad I was thinking of leaving, but he's been good to me so I thought I'd be honest with him.

"You have to go and live your life, Cassie. It'll be tough to replace you, but you and your girl deserve to be happy."

I could have kissed him.

Drawing in a deep breath, I dial Patrick.

It's midmorning, so I fully expect to have to leave him a voicemail. *Maybe I should have just sent a text.* Oh, who am I kidding? I need to hear his voice.

He's probably working anyway.

"Babe," he answers the phone, a smile in his voice.

"Oh. Hi. I wasn't sure if you'd answer."

"I'm on a break, and I always have time for you. What's going on?"

"I wondered if you might want a visitor for a few days." I smile.

"Does a bear shit in the woods? Just you? Or you and Sophie?"

"Lauren is coming to stay with Sophie. She's promised to behave, and Sophie will call me if there are any issues." I take a deep breath.

He chuckles. "You want to look at houses?"

"You said you had a few to view. If we're moving, I think it should be a joint decision."

"Of course. I wouldn't have bought one without your approval anyway. But it'll be nice—house shopping together."

I laugh. "I didn't know if I could trust you to do it alone."

"I'm wounded, Cassie. Deeply wounded."

"Oh, you big baby."

"I'm sure you can kiss me better."

A shiver runs through me. Me and Patrick having a few nights alone together. I can't wait to be with him again. Now we've resolved our past, we have our future to look forward to.

"Maybe. If you're lucky."

"When will you be here?"

"This afternoon." I draw in a deep breath. I'm so excited. For the first time in forever, it's nice to feel good about something.

"I've got back-to-back appointments this afternoon. But I

can leave a key with the receptionist here and you could pick it up?"

I grin. "That sounds great. I'll pick up the key and grab something for dinner."

"I'd rather have you."

"How about dinner and me?"

He laughs. "Even better. See you later. I love you."

"I love you too."

"That's the first time you've said it back."

I swallow hard. "Really?"

"I think you know it is. But it's okay if you've just caught up."

"I'm more than caught up. See you soon."

If Sophie was younger, I might hesitate, but I know my girl has her head screwed on right and she'll contact me if she needs to. Besides, I'm at most a couple of hours away and taking my own car—I can get back quickly if I need to.

I'm still nervous, but I have faith in my daughter and Lauren loves Sophie. The last thing she'd want to ever do is hurt her.

My bag's already packed—there was no way Patrick would say no. So it's a simple matter of throwing it in the back seat and then I'm driving away from the old and into the new.

It's terrifying and exciting all at once.

It's an easy drive in the middle of the day with light traffic, and my phone tells me where to go to find Patrick's offices.

I pull into a car park outside the building and make my way into a lovely air-conditioned office. The building is quiet, and the only person in the waiting room is a young woman whose gaze catches mine for a second before I reach the reception desk.

The receptionist smiles.

"Hi. I'm looking for Patrick Cross. He said he'd leave a key here for me."

She beams me a bright smile. "You must be Cassie."

"That's me."

"He talks about you a *lot*."

I laugh. "I hope not."

She plucks a key ring off a pile of papers and hands it to me.

"Thank you."

I turn to leave. A door clicks open behind me.

"Cassie."

I smile at Patrick's voice.

Turning back, I meet his gaze. "I thought you had an afternoon of appointments?"

"I do, but everything's running late today. But once I'm done, I'm all yours."

He kisses me tenderly on the lips. "I'm glad you're here."

"Me too. I'll get going and let you get back to work."

He nods. "I won't be late."

"I'll head to the supermarket first and grab something to cook for dinner."

His smile widens. "I'm looking forward to a home-cooked meal."

I peck him on the lips and walk away. "See you later."

Patrick won't be home for a few hours, so I have time to walk through a mall and see what I can find before heading to the supermarket. It's been a long time since I had time to myself and been somewhere I can shop up a storm. I'm not big on shopping, but I could do with some new clothes and things before the move. I'm making the most of having a clear out before we ship our things to Auckland.

I've been walking for about fifteen minutes when I'm sure I hear my name being called.

I look around, but no one seems familiar.

This is weird. I go back to looking at a dress in the doorway of a store when a hand brushes my arm.

"Cassie? Cassie Warren?"

Okay, that's weird.

My heart sinks as I turn around. "Vicki?"

She holds up her palms. "I'm probably the last person you'd ever want to see. But I've been trying to track you down for ages. We need to talk."

"I don't think I have anything to talk to you about."

In the years I knew Vicki, she was confident—full of herself.

This version looks unsure of herself. She reminds me of me back then.

"Please. I'll buy you a coffee?"

Curiosity gets the better of me and despite my better judgement, I nod.

"There's a coffee shop just over there in the middle of the mall."

I follow her. There's no bounce in her step the way there used to be. Her hair that was so perfectly coiffed is lank and hangs down over her shoulders.

This isn't the same woman who tormented me in school.

"What sort of coffee did you want?"

"Umm, a latte?"

She places an order and points at a table. I guess at least

we're in public and she can't prank me. I'm not sure why I even think about that after all these years—maybe it's engrained.

We sit at a table on opposite sides.

"So, how are you?"

I stare at her. "You wanted me here to ask me how I am?"

"No! I mean, yes, but there's more I want to say to you. Are you living in Auckland?"

I shake my head. "No, but I'm moving here soon."

She chews on her bottom lip a moment. "I'm sorry about your parents. I heard about the accident."

Interesting. If she'd still been in touch with Patrick then he'd have known about it too. I'm sure she wouldn't have been able to keep her mouth shut.

"Thank you."

The coffees arrive, and she dumps three spoons of sugar in it and gives it a stir.

Who is this woman?

"I really need to give up the coffee. I drink way too much of it. It doesn't help my nerves."

"I bet."

Her cheeks flush with colour. "We didn't sleep together that night. I was so upset and hurt that he dumped me— especially when it was you."

My brows rise.

"I mean, I knew if we split he'd go straight to you. He felt bad for a long time before the two of you got together for the way he'd left you behind when he started high school. But I think he felt stupid and didn't want to admit it. He got so angry when Dave helped pull that prank on you, and he punched him in the face over it."

I swallow hard. "I saw you two together."

She nods. "I uhh … do you remember Kelly Banks?"

I nod. She was one of Vicki's close friends and had her share of nasty remarks for me.

"Her mum was on Valium. We crushed one up and put it in Patrick's drink. He said he was waiting for you—I wasn't even invited. But by the time he realised I was there, he'd had his beer and was feeling tired. We helped him into bed."

My head swims. "Did you …"

"I never touched him. Not like that. We took his shirt off and pulled the covers over, and I got in with him. I took my top off. We were fully clothed underneath the covers. I just wanted to hurt you."

"We broke up over it."

Guilt swamps her features. "Dave said he saw you that night and how upset you were. He was so angry at me when I told him what I'd done."

Tears prick my eyes.

"I married him." She drops her gaze to her coffee. "He cheated on me."

For a moment, I don't know what to say. "I'm sorry to hear that."

She smiles at me, but it's forced. "You don't have to say that. I wouldn't feel sorry for me if I were you."

"But I know how it feels. Patrick might not have cheated on me, but I thought he did. And it broke my heart. Did you have kids?"

She nods, and my heart aches on her behalf. "Two. He left and didn't look back. I've been chasing him for child support for years."

"I always knew he was useless."

Vicki snorts. "You're not wrong. What about you?"

My throat tightens. "I was pregnant when Patrick and I split. But I didn't know."

Her mouth falls open. "Oh, God. I'm so sorry."

"It's a long story, but we found our way back to each other. We've got a fourteen-year-old daughter."

"How long were you apart?" The pain in her eyes is unbearable.

I almost wish I hadn't dropped that on her.

"We just got back together recently. I've been living in Hamilton. I'm up here for a few days while we look at houses so Sophie and I can move."

Her smile seems more genuine this time. "I'm happy for you."

"Thank you. I hope you have more luck extracting money from Dave."

She rolls her eyes. "I'm not counting on it. But I've got my kids and we're doing okay. It's not easy, but I don't have to deal with his bullshit anymore."

That makes *me* snort. And I clamp my hand over my nose in shock.

"I'm so sorry, Cassie. When things got bad with Dave, I was so far in over my head and I felt so bad about what I'd done. But you'd moved and I didn't know where you were."

I take a sip of my coffee. "How did you end up here?"

"We moved before Dave decided the grass was greener. Cheated on me with a twenty-one-year-old. God only knows what she saw in him. Maybe she thought he was wealthy, but that's a joke. They're not together now."

"He was always such a dick."

She nods. "I didn't see it for the longest time. It made me

realise how lucky I was to have Patrick for as long as I did, but I think he was really always yours."

Finding out what happened that night is good, but I do actually feel sorry for her. She's got nothing, and I have everything.

Speaking to her just emphasises the fact that I've made the right decision.

I can't wait to tell Patrick.

———

I'm at the stove stirring pasta when Patrick walks in the door.

"Did you have a good day?"

He slips his arms around my waist and nuzzles my neck. "Not bad. Coming home is the best part."

"I started looking at houses online. But I don't know what budget we're looking at, and they're all out of my price range."

He takes a step back and moves to my side. "We're doing this together. I have a deposit in my savings, and I bought this place a few years ago when apartments were cheaper, so I can sell this."

I nod. "I still have the proceeds of the sale of my parents' house. They had a mortgage, but there wasn't a huge amount left, so that's been my nest egg for all these years. I'd like to keep Gran's place—I thought I could rent it out while I take my time to find a job here." Turning the element off, I breathe in the tomato pasta sauce.

"That smells amazing. I can't wait," Patrick says.

"How about you take a seat and I'll bring it to you?" I place a gentle kiss on his lips.

"Okay, but tomorrow I'll take care of the dinner and the pampering."

"Sounds good to me."

I plate the two meals and carry them into the living room. The news is on the television in the background, and I take a seat next to him on the couch and hand him his plate.

"This feels very … domestic." He smiles.

"Your apartment's nice. Shame it's not bigger."

"Do you really want to live in an apartment?"

I lean back and shrug. "Right now I'd be happy that we're all together."

We eat in silence and when we're done, I collect his plate despite his protests and rinse them both off before putting them in the dishwasher.

After pouring two glasses of wine, I return to the living room, placing the glasses on the coffee table.

"I ran into Vicki this afternoon."

He frowns. "Vicki?"

"Vicki as in your ex-girlfriend?"

Patrick snorts. "What the hell? Of all the people you could meet."

"I know. It really is a small world."

He leans back on the couch. "I bet that was fun."

I drop onto the couch beside him and snuggle against his side. He wraps one arm around me and pulls me closer.

"It was educational. I know what happened the night of the party now."

His eyes search mine. "You spoke about it?"

"She brought it up." I bite my bottom lip. "You didn't

cheat on me. I know we already decided that something went on, but it turns out that she put Kelly's mother's Valium in your drink. You got sleepy and she set the whole thing up."

Patrick's mouth falls open. "She drugged me?"

"Clearly it didn't completely knock you out, but it does explain why your eyes were glazed over. I thought it was the alcohol."

"I had one drink."

"I thought you could be lying." Tears prick my eyes. "I'm sorry."

"No, you had no idea." He cups my cheek. "I wish you hadn't gone through that."

"We're together now."

Patrick presses his forehead to mine. "We are, and once we get this house, I want to make that permanent."

"Yes," I whisper.

"Did you say yes?" he asks.

"I did. Sophie agrees with me."

The next few moments are a blur as he kisses me long and hard.

"Thank you, Cassie."

"What for?"

"For loving me even when you thought you had no reason to. For having faith in me regardless of the past. For being here with me when all I need is you and Sophie. For the next few nights, you're all mine. We'll see if we can find our dream home and then bring our girl to see it. I wish she could be here too."

I lean my head against his. "If we don't find anything while I'm here, we can both come up for the school holidays."

He strokes my hair, and I close my eyes.

"I'd like that. The sooner we're all under one roof, the better."

He kisses me softly.

"Today when I came in, who was that woman in the waiting room? She gave me a weird look."

He sighs. "A patient. She got too attached, so Ethan's taken over her last surgery. But I'm thinking we should have transferred her somewhere else so she wouldn't be in our building."

"Does that happen often?"

Patrick shakes his head. "Most of the time, it's a one-off. Something that needs to be corrected or a reconstruction. But her case involved multiple consultations and more than one surgery, so I became a bit of a regular part of her life for a while."

I reach up and cup his cheek. "You are rather gorgeous."

He laughs and turns his head to kiss my palm. "I only worry about what you think."

"You're as hot as you were when we were at school."

Patrick squeezes me against him. "You are even more beautiful."

"Flatterer."

He shakes his head. "Just a man in love."

34

CASSIE

The third house we look at—I fall in love.

It's a four bedroom with plenty of backyard space. Not too far from Patrick's work, but any closer and the price would shoot up.

As it is, buying a house in Auckland isn't cheap. But if we pool the funds we have, and based on Patrick's salary, we can do it.

I stand in the spacious kitchen, marvelling at the sun shining through the sliding doors out to the deck. "This is going to be lovely in the mornings."

"You want it?"

I nod. "I want to try."

Patrick grins and kisses me while the real estate agent's cheeks redden and she looks away.

"I've already got pre-approval from the bank even without your money. I did that first, so I knew roughly how much."

"We can make an offer?"

He slips his arms around my waist. "We can make an offer."

When we're out in the car, he gives me a tentative look. "I thought we could go and see my parents this afternoon. I haven't told them anything about your parents. I thought we'd do it all together."

My chest tightens. I hate talking about them, but I understand why he's held back. Talking about it might help Mrs Cross understand everything I've been through.

We'll have to tell them why we broke up and about Sophie.

Oh, Sophie.

Telling the Crosses still makes me nervous. I'm not sure how I'd feel if someone turned up years after the fact and announced they'd given birth to my grandchild.

"What do you think? We don't have to, but I think the sooner we rip off the band-aid the better."

I nod. "Let's get this over with."

The drive out there is long but scenic. I hate traveling, but I do like being out in the country with the fresh air and seeing the green fields.

He pulls down the driveway of a beautiful country house.

Anxiety builds in my chest, but Patrick reaches across and takes my hand in his. "It'll be fine, Cassie. Trust me?"

"I trust you. I just don't know ..."

Mrs Cross is out the front of the house, on her knees in the garden. She looks up as we exit the car and it takes her about a second to clock me.

"Patrick." She smiles warmly at him, barely giving me a glance.

He walks around to my side of the car, slipping his arm around my waist. It's a simple act of solidarity, but with it, I steel my spine.

"Mum, you remember Cassie?"

"Of course I do," she snaps.

He gives my waist a squeeze. "We have some news."

She rolls her eyes before turning and walking toward the house. "Come on. I'll put on the jug. Your father's inside."

We trail along behind her, stopping only to take off our shoes on the mat outside.

Inside the house is lovely.

They're obviously very proud of Patrick, the entranceway walls covered with photos and Patrick's achievements.

Maybe this was a mistake, but it's too late now.

"Cassie." Patrick's father, Brian, opens his arms and I give him a brief hug before stepping back. I don't miss Jane glaring at him, but I keep my focus on his warm smile. "How have you been, love? Keeping well?"

"Not too bad. Thanks for asking."

"And how are your mum and dad?"

I knew that they didn't know about my parents, but the question still hits me like a sledgehammer. My eyes well with tears.

Brian frowns. "Are you okay, sweetheart?"

Patrick reaches for my hand and gives it a squeeze. "Actually, Dad …"

"They died," I croak.

Jane shares a worried look with her husband. "Oh, Cassie. I'll get that coffee sorted and we'll have a chat."

I nod. Patrick leads me to the couch while his father sits back in his chair.

The silence is awkward until Jane returns with the coffee.

She takes a seat and gives me a small smile.

Patrick leans in. "Tell them."

I nod. "A couple of weeks after you left, we were in a car accident. I was the only survivor."

Jane gasps.

"I'm so sorry to her that. Your parents were lovely people," Brian says.

"Cassie was badly hurt." Patrick squeezes my knee.

Any judgement on Jane's face is gone. The sympathy in her expression is almost enough to make me cry.

"I broke both my legs and fractured my spine in two places. There were multiple surgeries to put me back together."

She shakes her head. "I wish we'd known."

"I moved to Hamilton with my grandmother, and that's where I am now."

Jane arches an eyebrow. "That explains Patrick being away so much."

"There's something else we need to tell you." Patrick slips an arm around my shoulders and tugs me close.

I meet his gaze and shake my head. It's his news for his parents—not my place to tell them. I know he thinks it'll bring us closer, but I'm really not sure how they'll take news of grandchild who's just turned fourteen.

"Cassie was pregnant at the time of the accident."

Brian and Jane exchange a worried look.

"What I'm trying to tell you is that you have a fourteen-year-old granddaughter."

That hard look is back in Jane's eyes.

Brian claps his hands together. "That's wonderful. Tell us all about her."

"Her name is Sophie. Cassie spent her pregnancy and Sophie's early years having surgeries and getting things back on track. But we're together now and working on what our next move is going to be."

Jane clears her throat. "Do you have a picture?"

Patrick pulls out his phone. "A ton of them." He navigates to his Sophie folder and hands her the phone. "Scroll through these."

She takes it from him and flicks between the photos, Brian watching over her shoulder.

"She's beautiful." There's warmth in her voice now. She must have a lot of questions, but in this moment, she's looking at Sophie's picture with all the love of a grand-mother. "When can we meet her?"

"Soon," Patrick says. "We're working through things now. Cassie's here to help me find a home for us."

Her eyes light up. "Really? You're moving to Auckland?"

I nod. "We are. Patrick and I found a house today that we like and once we've got a place to live, we'll move up."

"She looks so much like you, Cassie," Brian says.

I smile at Patrick. "I see both of us in her."

"Will you two stay for dinner?"

Jane's question hangs in the air, and Patrick gives me the 'What do you think?' look.

I nod.

"Sure," he says. "We'd like that."

For the next couple of hours we talk. Most of it is about Sophie—it turns out she's the perfect subject to fill the conversation with. And I don't mind that because I love talking about my girl.

Patrick insists on helping his mother with dinner so I can talk to his dad. Most of that conversation is reminiscing over the past and remembering my parents. The more I talk, the more comfortable I am.

I've never had that before—speaking with people who actually knew them. Once I moved to Gran's, I didn't talk to anyone back home.

Dinner's conversation is about the future—the house we hope to buy and our plans which are limited but growing by the minute.

And when Patrick goes out the back with his father, who wants to show him the new things he's growing in his vege patch, Jane corners me.

"You hurt him so badly," she says.

I'm not sure I can handle this hot and cold act with her.

"He hurt me. I thought he'd cheated."

The colour drains from her face. "What?"

"The party he had before you moved—I caught him in bed with Vicki."

She's gobsmacked. Her mouth forms an 'O' as she stares at me. "What?"

"Patrick and I just found out the whole story. Vicki and one her friends put something in his beer to make him sleepy and then staged the whole thing. She was so nasty. She made me think that he'd been stringing me along for a bet."

Jane just blinks rapidly.

"I had no idea. We were just kids. And then you left …"

"And then you had the accident, and the baby, and …"

"Exactly. I did try one day to come and tell Patrick, but I saw him with another girl and I thought he'd moved on." Tears prick my eyes.

"Oh, sweetheart. I'm so sorry. It sounds like everything just went badly and you had no one but your grandmother. Am I right?"

I nod. "I was mess too. After Sophie was born, it all came crashing down and it took me a while to get on top of that. But meeting Patrick again after all these years—I think things are finally going to work out."

Her lips purse. "I won't pretend that I wasn't angry. But it seems like a lot of that was misplaced. I want you to know that I'm here for you. And for Sophie."

I smile. "Thank you. I was scared about coming here today, but Patrick said you'd be over the moon finding out about your granddaughter." I pause for a moment. "Patrick didn't tell you, but her middle name is Jane."

She presses her hand to her heart, emotion swimming in her eyes. "It is?"

"I wanted her to have a link to your family."

Her lips curl until she's smiling too. "Thank you. It's a shock and a lot to take in, but I'm so proud of you, Cassie. You've battled through so much and come out the other side, and from what Patrick said, you've raised a wonderful girl. I can't wait to meet her."

"We'll have to make that happen soon."

35

CASSIE

The past few weeks have been hectic.

Our offer was snapped up for the house, and the owners wanted a fast settlement date as they're leaving the country.

We weren't saying no to that.

My plan to rent out Gran's place is going ahead. We're leaving it partially furnished so we don't have to move everything—besides, we bought new things for the new house like beds and a lounge suite.

The movers emptied the house today, but the way we've organised things mean we've got beds to sleep in tonight.

Tomorrow we start our new life, and it's been a long time since I've been so happy.

Patrick slides his arm around me, becoming the big spoon and I settle back against his hard chest.

"I love you, Cassie," he whispers.

"I love you too."

I'm so tired from packing that it's not long before I'm drifting off.

Mark's always in the back of my mind. We'll always have the memories of the years we lived here, but this was where his journey ended.

And I'm okay with that.

Mark walks toward me with open arms, and I fall into them.

"I've missed you," I whisper.

"I love you. But you need to wake up and get out."

"No. I don't want to leave you."

He smiles, and it's soft and loving. "You belong with Patrick. You know that. I'll never stop loving you, Cassie, but you need to go."

A screeching sound pierces my hearing.

My eyes fly open.

Smoke fills the room, and I look to my left. Patrick's only a second behind me, springing up and out of bed.

"We've got to get out of here," he yells.

"Sophie."

"I'm here, Mum." Sophie's voice comes from the hallway, and without another thought, we all run through the living room to the front door.

The sound of sirens fills the air—someone must have noticed and called them already—and when we run onto front lawn, I turn and press my hand to my chest.

My grandmother's house is on fire.

I don't even realise I'm shivering until the warmth of a blanket is draped over my shoulders. Mrs McIntyre stands behind me with another in her hands for Sophie.

"Someone was in your backyard. I called the police. Then

I saw flames and called the fire service. Sounds like they're on their way."

This all reminds me of the day Mark died.

Everything happens around me.

I hold my daughter close as the firefighters get to work. I'm only grateful that the house was nearly empty and we all got out.

A small crowd gathers on the footpath to watch. Two police cars pull up, and officers start getting out.

"Patrick?"

A young woman's voice comes from the crowd, and we all turn toward it.

"Emily?" He gives my hand a squeeze. "What are you doing here?"

She pales. "I didn't … I didn't know you were in the house. I just wanted to scare her away."

My throat tightens.

"Are you saying you lit the fire?" he asks.

She glances at me. "You're not supposed to be with *her*."

Patrick pulls me close and waves to one of the police officers. They've been taking statements given someone was seen running from the place, but I think we just found her.

The female officer approaches, and Patrick recounts the conversation.

She turns toward Emily and guides her away from us.

We watch from a distance.

I swallow hard as they arrest her. She goes limp when they put her in the back of the police car and dips her head as they drive away.

"Are you okay?" Patrick asks.

"She was at your office the day I came to get the key to your apartment."

He presses a kiss to my temple. "I'm so sorry I put you at risk."

"It's not your fault. How were you to know she'd do something like that?"

Patrick sighs. "I knew she had attachment issues. A colleague took over her case. Apparently, none of us realised how serious it was."

"Is there anyone you want us to call?" another of the police officers asks us.

"We should call Lauren. Maybe we can stay there tonight."

I nod and give them Lauren's number.

I feel bad that I'm not calling her—she'll freak out at the idea of losing me and Sophie. But it can't be helped.

"If you want to come with me, I'll drive you to her place," the officer says. "She's waiting."

I look back at Patrick.

"I'll stay here for a bit. Hopefully I can get in and get some of our things and secure the place for the night."

"Are you sure you don't want us here?"

He shakes his head and brushes a lock of hair behind my ear. "No, I want you and our daughter to be safe and get some sleep. Lauren will be worried about you."

"I won't sleep until you're there."

Patrick kisses my cheek. "I bet by the time you've had a shower and a hot drink, you'll be fast asleep in no time. At least the house was nearly empty."

I nod. "I keep thinking about all the things we could have lost."

"Ms Warren?"

I turn toward the police car. Sophie's sitting in the back seat, and I force a smile at the police officer waiting.

"I'm on my way." I give Patrick's hand a squeeze. "Call me if you need to."

Despite thinking I won't sleep, I'm dead on my feet by the time we get to Lauren's.

When we walk in the front door, I pull Sophie into my arms and close my eyes. Tonight could have ended in disaster. Thank God for smoke alarms and dreams of Mark.

"I've got some of my clothes for both of you to change into," Lauren says. "There were a few things Mark left that Patrick can use for the night."

"Thank you, Lauren."

She flashes me a faint smile. "I'm just glad you're all safe. You can have Mark's room—I figured you'd want to stick together and his bed's big enough for the three of you."

"I appreciate it." Tears well in my eyes.

"Go get in the shower," she says to Sophie. "There are pyjamas at the end of Mark's bed."

She pulls away from me, but I don't want to let her go at first.

"Mum, I'm okay."

I press a kiss in her hair. All I can smell is smoke. "Go."

As she walks away, I turn to Lauren.

"I'd hug you, but all I can smell is smoke. You can use my ensuite if you want a shower too."

"Oh, I'd love that. Are you sure?"

"Of course. I'm just so happy to see you. I'm not sure I could cope with losing you two."

I give her forearm a squeeze. "I'll go and have that shower and come back. Put the jug on."

After heading up the stairs, I go through Lauren's room to her ensuite.

The hot water is reassuring. The clothes, I think I'm going to have to throw out as I'm not sure about getting the smoky smell out of them.

But that's a problem for another day.

When I'm finished, I wrap a towel around me and head to Mark's room. There's a pair of pyjamas on the end of the bed, and Sophie's fast asleep.

God, how I love this kid.

I sit beside her and scrape her hair back that's fallen on her face. It's still damp and it'll need a good brush in the morning, but that's the least of our worries tonight.

She's alive and well, and we're all okay.

I place a kiss on her temple and turn out the light as I leave.

Lauren's waiting downstairs when I return with a hot mug of coffee, and I join her in the living room.

"She's already asleep." I cradle my drink in my hands. "Oh, Lauren. I keep thinking about how I could have lost her tonight. Or Patrick. Or both."

"Thank God you're all safe. I know you were heading to Auckland tomorrow, but you're welcome to stay here as long as you need to."

I nod absently. "Mark was looking out for us tonight."

Her brows knit. "What do you mean?"

"I dreamed of him. That's happened a couple of times since he died, but it felt like a warning. The alarms woke me, but he was telling me in my dream to get out."

She nods. "That would be so him. He really loved you and Sophie. I don't know what I would have done if anything had happened to you."

"I just can't believe it. Some jealous young woman trying to warn me away from Patrick. Even if we can rebuild, the house will never be the same."

Lauren moves closer and lays her hand on my forearm. "I know dealing with the house is an added complication, but maybe it is a sign that you're doing the right thing—getting a fresh start away from here."

"You should come with us. This place is no good for you."

She sighs. "Sometimes I feel like the memories will drown me."

"When we're settled, come and stay. Look around and see if there's something for you."

"I don't want to impose when you're starting a new life as a family."

"You *are* family, Lauren. You're the sister I never had."

I place my mug on the table, and she does the same.

She reaches for me, and I pull her into a hug. "Sophie and I love you so much. Please take care of yourself."

"I'm trying," she whispers.

"Then think about coming to see us. We'd love to have you. Maybe this is your chance for a fresh start too."

"Okay."

We just sit for a while, and I'm so grateful for this woman coming into my life. She was the bonus that arrived with Mark, and I'm not going to let her go any time soon.

We're tied together for life.

"I should get some sleep," I finally say. "I don't know when Patrick will get here."

"I'll stay here and mind the fort." She smiles. "I won't sleep until you're all under this roof anyway."

"Are you sure?"

Lauren nods. "Go to bed, Cassie. I'll send him up when he gets here."

I mount the stairs, weariness in every step, and climb into bed beside my daughter.

For a few minutes, I study her in her sleep.

We've been through so much, and I couldn't be more proud of how brave and strong she is.

I close my eyes, but sleep eludes me.

I'm not sure how long it is before Patrick slips into the room and gets into bed behind me. He smells fresh from the shower, and I breathe a sigh of relief as his arm reaches over me and Sophie.

He kisses the back of my neck.

"Is everything okay?" I murmur.

"You're still awake?"

"I couldn't sleep until you were here." I roll over to face him.

"The house is secured. Thankfully because your neighbours called quickly, the fire damage is restricted to the back of the house. But there'll be smoke damage too." He places a kiss on my forehead. "But the two most precious things in my life are safe, and I'm thankful for that."

"I'm glad our personal things were already with the movers."

He sighs. "That too. I brought your handbag and the suitcases you had packed. I can't believe Emily did this. I'm so sorry, Cassie."

"It's not your fault. At least they caught the person who did it."

"I'll call Ethan in the morning and let him know what's happened. If it's okay with Lauren we'll stay here a few days so we can meet with the insurance assessors or whoever else we need to deal with."

I nod. "So much for a good start to our new life."

"Hey," he says softly. "We're all alive and we're together. That's what's important. If anything happened to either of you, I wouldn't be able to live with myself."

Tears well in my eyes.

"I love you and Sophie with everything I have. You're my whole life."

He gathers me into his arms and I fall asleep breathing him in—finally feeling safe again.

CASSIE

Three months.

That's all it took for us to be living with Patrick and for him to get me pregnant again.

Contraception and us don't seem to work well together.

I sit on the toilet seat, the third test I've taken in my hands. Like the other two tests, two pink lines show me the undeniable truth.

As much as I've always wanted Sophie to have siblings, I thought we had a little more time.

When the front door opens and closes, I pinch the bridge of my nose.

It's the same routine every day.

Patrick walks in the door, and Sophie goes flying into his arms. The two of them are rapidly making up for lost time, and although the guilt still weighs on me over keeping them apart, both reassure me they don't resent me.

His heavy footsteps on the stairs tell me she's sent him

my way. Not wanting to tell her what I was doing, I'd feigned a headache to come up to our bedroom to lie down.

When he taps on the door, I sigh.

"Come in."

His eyebrows are raised as he takes in the sight of me sitting on the toilet, lid down.

"Are you okay? Sophie said you weren't feeling well. Another headache?"

I nod. "I'll be fine. It's a bit more serious than a headache though."

He frowns. "More serious? Babe? What's going on?"

I hand him the pregnancy test. "About eighteen years of serious."

Patrick stares at the test for a moment before a smile spreads across that smarmy face of his. Trust him to be proud of what he's done. "We're having a baby?"

"You're the doctor. You tell me." I can't stop my lips from curling into a smile that matches his.

He casts his gaze across the vanity where the other two tests lie. "Well, in my professional opinion, testing three times is crazy but probably a more reliable indication than one positive test."

I bark out a laugh. "You're such a dick sometimes."

"But you love me." He squats in front of me. "Are you okay with this?"

"Do I have a choice?"

He reaches up and pushes my hair back behind my ear. "You always have a choice. But I'm very excited if you want to have a baby with me."

"I didn't think it would happen so fast, but I'd really love to have a baby with you."

Patrick looks around. "Could we move this somewhere other than the toilet?"

I laugh and push myself to my feet. "Lie down with me?"

He nods, rising to meet my gaze. "I'd like that. Sophie thinks you're lying down anyway, and I'll just order takeout tonight."

"That sounds good. I don't feel like cooking."

"Me either. I feel like celebrating."

"You're really happy?"

"Cassie. I wish I hadn't missed out on you being pregnant with Sophie, but I did. And there's nothing either of us can do to change that. This time. I'll be right here going through it with you."

Tears prick my eyes. "Yes. We'll do it together."

He leans in, pressing his forehead to mine. "I know it's earlier than we talked about, but it's meant to be."

Taking my hand in his, he leads me into our room and toward our bed.

I lie down on top of the duvet, resting my head on the cool pillow. Patrick kicks off his shoes and climbs up beside me, spooning me, his hand resting on my stomach. He makes me feel safe as he always does, the warmth of him radiating through me.

Any anxiousness I felt when I first saw the two lines pop up has gone. Am I still worried about this being too early in our new relationship for this? Maybe. But Patrick has my back and won't let me down.

From the moment we met again at the hospital, he's been steadfast in his support. He was patient and there for me even when I wasn't sure I wanted him to be.

I'm more in love with him than I've ever been.

That scares me sometimes—I haven't forgotten my prior heartbreak.

But we're both adults now and this is a whole different kind of relationship than it was back then when I was a girl —giddy that the boy she always loved was interested in her.

And now I have him for life.

"Marry me," he whispers.

"What are you talking about?" I roll over to face him.

"If we hadn't broken up, we'd be married and celebrating our anniversaries every year with our children. Let's do this before this baby's born."

I slip my arms around his neck. "I didn't know you were so traditional."

He chuckles. "I'm not, but I think it's the perfect time. We'll invite Lauren up here to spend some time with us and get her out of that house, have a wedding in our amazing backyard, and move back on the course we were always meant to be on."

"We could change Sophie's name."

He nods. "I have been meaning to talk to you about that, but I didn't want to push."

"If I'm going to be a Cross, then she needs to be too."

His eyebrows rise. "Is that a yes?"

"It's a yes, Patrick Cross."

37

CASSIE

It doesn't take long to pull a wedding together.

By myself it might have, but Jane and Brian were over the moon, and once Lauren found out, we had more help than we knew what to do with.

It'll be a quiet affair—just our family and Patrick's friend, Ethan.

Sophie and I will be walking down the aisle together. It felt right for the three of us to be part of the ceremony. Well, four if you count the little nugget I'm carrying.

"Mum, are you ready?"

I found the perfect dress at the bridal shop, but I balked at the price until Patrick stepped in and told me to spend the money. It's long and flowing in an off-white soft fabric that feels like a dream to wear.

"I am." I turn to take in the sight of my daughter.

Her dress is blue and matches her eyes. It's the first time

she's worn a gown, and she looks much older than her fourteen years.

"Look at you. So grown up."

I open my arms, and she snuggles in against me.

"Let's get you married to Dad."

"Okay, okay, Sophie Cross."

She grins. The name change took about three weeks, and she was over the moon to share her father's name. After today, it'll be my name too.

"I love you, Mum."

"I love you too. So very much."

She takes my hand, and we walk down the stairs and to the back door.

Patrick's waiting under a tree near the back of the lawn, and together we make our way to him.

His mouth falls open.

And all I see is him.

When we reach him, he gives Sophie a kiss and she goes and sits with Lauren.

Patrick takes my hand in his.

I'm so busy looking into his eyes, I barely hear the first part of the ceremony until we reach the vows.

"Cassie. You were always the one. Even when you thought you weren't and we were apart, it was always you. My heart and my life are yours, and you and Sophie fill them every day with your love. You're my soul mate—my everything. I love you."

I blow out a breath and drop Patrick's hands for a moment to swipe away tears on my cheeks.

He takes my hands in his again. "Your turn," he whispers.

I lick my lips, my mouth suddenly dry. For so long, I

didn't dare to dream about this moment, and now it's real and happening.

"Patrick. You are my everything. You're my best friend, my rock, my heart—everything I am. Today we finally become one and will be for the rest of our lives. I can't wait for us to start our life together with our children. I look forward to growing old with you."

When the celebrant declares us married, he dips me and gives me a long kiss as everyone claps and cheers.

"Got you, Cassie," he whispers.

"For always."

After what feels like a million photos, we move onto a barbecue in the backyard with the people we love.

I nudge Patrick's arm. "Look at that."

Lauren's laughter rings out across the yard as Ethan tells her a story that has him animated.

Patrick's parents are engrossed in something Sophie's saying—that kid has her grandparents wrapped around her little finger.

"I love our life," he says.

I grip his hand. "Me too. I love this house. I love that we're having a child here and we're growing our family. I love you." I reach up and touch his cheek.

He leans down and kisses me long and slow.

"Get a room, you guys," Ethan calls.

"We've got one." Patrick laughs.

38

PATRICK

In the months that followed our wedding, things just got better and better.

I get to be a part of this pregnancy and watch Cassie bloom.

It's not all fun. She has more than her share of morning sickness, but I'm glad that I can give her the type of lifestyle where she doesn't have to rush to find a job. I don't really care if she never bothers looking.

As far as I'm concerned, she's done the hard yards all this time for our girl, and now I get to pamper both of them. And soon, the three of them.

Of course we're having another girl.

Cassie leans back in her chair after dinner and sighs. She's two weeks off her due date and has never been more beautiful.

"Are you okay?" I ask.

"No, I should have bought donuts with the groceries. I'd kill one right now."

Sophie laughs. "We should go to Dunkin', Dad. Get a half dozen."

Cassie presses her hands together and does those puppy dog eyes I can never resist. "Please? Could you?"

I laugh. "Anything for you. Do you want to come for a ride?"

"No, I want to flop on the couch and not move for the rest of the night."

I get up and round the table to give her a kiss. "Fair enough. Want some help?"

"Thanks. I'm sure I can waddle over there. Might need some help getting out of this chair, though."

"You're such a drama queen, Mum." Sophie rolls her eyes.

"I'm allowed to be."

After I've made sure Cassie's safely on the couch, I turn toward Sophie.

"Dad, come on."

I smile. That'll never get old. When I first laid eyes on Sophie, I knew, but hearing her call me Dad makes everything alright with the world.

Getting Cassie back is the best thing that ever happened to me.

Sophie is the icing on the top.

I'm so determined never to miss a second of this new baby's life. It'd be easy to resent Cassie for keeping Sophie from me, but we wouldn't have the life we do now if I let it eat me up.

"You know I'm not as fast as you. It's old age."

"You're not *that* old."

I turn back to Cassie. "I'll have my phone on me. Call me if you need anything."

She rubs her belly. "Get me my sugar fix and I'll be happy."

I laugh. "Okay, okay."

After grabbing my keys from the kitchen bench, I make my way out to my car, Sophie right behind me.

It's not a long drive—maybe ten minutes or so—and Sophie talks the whole way. She's so excited about having a sibling.

I'm relieved to get there. The sooner we're done, the sooner we can get out of here.

I jump out of the car and go in.

Of course there are a million donuts and I didn't ask Cassie what she wanted.

The girl behind the counter leans forward. "Which flavours were you after?"

I'm so busy focused on the donuts, that Sophie's elbow to the ribs comes as a surprise. "Ouch. What are you doing?"

She rolls her eyes and tilts her head toward the woman behind the counter.

I shrug. "What flavour would your mother want?"

Sophie laughs. She has dimples in her cheeks like I do when I do that, and it distracts me for a moment.

God how I love my kid.

"For someone so smart, you're so not observant."

"Give me a break. These all look good."

"I'm not talking about the donuts, Dad."

"I have no idea what you're talking about, but please tell me what your mother likes. I'll look like an idiot if I have to call her."

She laughs even harder. "She likes the jam-filled ones. Just get her a couple of those. And maybe some with sprinkles on."

I place the order and the woman fills the box with the ones we think Cassie will like.

After paying, I turn away and walk out to the car.

When we're inside, Sophie pinches my arm.

"That lady in there was flirting with you." She giggles. "It was hilarious. You were completely oblivious."

I laugh. "Was she? This is going to sound clichéd, but I don't notice anyone but your mother."

She beams a smile at me that warms my heart. "I love how much you love her. Dad … I mean, Mark did too. She deserves it."

"You can still call him Dad you know."

Sophie's brows knit. "I just wasn't sure. Because when you weren't with us, he was my dad."

"He was a good man, Soph. And he loved you when I couldn't. I don't mind at all."

She bites her bottom lip. "I'm happy you and Mum are having a baby."

"You know we'll both love you just as much, don't you?"

While she nods, there's uncertainty in her eyes.

I grasp her forearm so she meets my gaze.

"I know I missed out on your early years, but you are my daughter. And I couldn't be happier to have you in my life or more proud of you. I love you, Sophie Jane Cross."

A smile crosses her lips. "I love you too, Dad."

"Let's get these donuts back to your mother. I'm sure she's looking forward to the sugar rush."

She giggles and nods.

I put the key in the ignition and start the car before bucking up my seatbelt and glancing over at Sophie to make sure she's done the same.

She reaches over and picks up my phone. "The screen just lit up."

After tapping in my code, she scans the screen and her eyes widen. "Mum's been trying to call. There's like a kajillion missed calls."

Shit.

"I think she started when we went in for donuts."

I breathe a sigh of relief. It's maybe fifteen minutes that I've been without it. "Let's get going. You call her back."

Sophie holds the phone to her ear.

I have to focus. Pulling out into the traffic, I do my best not to panic. This isn't like Cassie.

"She's not answering."

"We'll be there soon."

I wind my way through the streets to get home. Thankfully we're not too far away, and we soon pull into the driveway.

Sophie and I jump out of the car and run toward the house.

Cassie's where I left her—lying on the couch—but her face is flushed with colour and she's gritting her teeth.

A dark pool of something wet is on the carpet.

"Cass. I'm so sorry. I left the phone in the car while we got the donuts. What's going on?"

"I called an ambulance. I'm sorry. I wasn't sure if I could wait," she sobs.

"It's okay." I stroke her cheek with my fingertips. "I'm here now."

It's a rush thinking of my medical training. I've delivered a baby or two when I was a junior doctor, but it's been a while.

I've got to be calm for Cassie.

"Sophie, can you get some towels from the linen cupboard?"

She nods and shoots up the stairs.

"Let me examine you." I give Cassie's hand a squeeze and help her out of her wet clothing.

I close my eyes when I realise just how close she is. "This little lady's grown impatient."

"I know second babies can come faster."

I nod. "Our daughter wants out."

Sophie comes back and I unfold a towel and slip it under Cassie. It's not perfect, but it should help make her more comfortable.

"Next contraction, if you feel like it, push. Okay?"

Cassie nods.

It only takes a moment before she's gritting her teeth and baring down.

"I see the head, babe. You're doing so well."

"It hurts."

"I know. But you can do it. I know you can. It's not going to take much this time."

The next time she pushes, we get a little further.

Noise happens behind me. The front door opens and closes. But I'm focused on my wife and baby.

A hand grips my shoulder.

"We can take over," a paramedic says.

I meet Cassie's gaze, and she shakes her head.

"Not a chance. I'm looking forward to meeting my baby girl. She's crowning, and I think one more push will do it."

Cassie nods, her face contorting with pain.

"When it comes, babe. I love you."

"I love you too." She closes her eyes a moment before she bears down one last time.

"Big push, Cass. You can do it."

"Go, Mum."

I bite down a smile as Sophie cheers Cassie on in the background. This was not the plan at all, but I'm grateful that while it's been a rush, it'll be over for Cassie soon. I hate seeing her in pain.

With a big push, the baby's shoulders are out and the rest of her slips into my arms. I breathe a sigh of relief as I check her over and she lets out an almighty wail.

The paramedic speaks up beside me. "I can deal with the placenta if you want."

I nod. "That would be good."

By the time the cord is cut and the placenta delivered, Cassie's lying exhausted against the couch cushions, and I gently place the baby against her chest before we cover her with warm towels.

"I'm sorry you couldn't get hold of me." I plant a kiss on her forehead.

"It was just all so sudden."

"That's more common after the first baby. I should have been more prepared."

Cassie strokes the baby's head. "She was just impatient—she is early."

"Thankfully not too early. I'll get you to bed after this."

"Do you want me to call Nana?" Sophie asks.

I meet Cassie's gaze, and she nods. "I'd like that."

Their relationship isn't perfect, but Mum got over her anger about the past once she found out what really happened. I know she'll step in and help without crossing any boundaries or getting in Cassie's way.

We'd talked about her coming to stay for a week or so after the baby was born, but we didn't plan on anything happening early—which was probably naive of us.

I sit beside the couch and hug Cassie. "I'm so proud of you."

"Did you want to go to hospital, Mrs Cross?"

Cassie grimaces. "Do I have to?"

The paramedic smiles. "Not if you don't want to. Everything's looking good."

"We'll be okay. I'm right here," I say.

"Congratulations, Mr and Mrs Cross." The paramedics make their way out, and then we're alone.

Cassie strokes our daughter's face. The baby's perfect. She's so much like Sophie was at birth from the photos I've seen—dark hair and blue eyes.

"Charlotte Lauren."

I nod. "I love it. Lauren will love it too."

She swallows hard. "I miss her."

My lips twitch, and I can't stop the smile that spreads across them. "Between you and me, I think she'll be up here before too long."

Cassie's brows rise. "Really?"

"She and Ethan … I'm not sure how serious it is yet, but he's done for."

She smiles a hazy smile. "I'm happy for both of them. Lauren deserves someone who will really love her."

"I think so too. And he's a good man." I kiss her temple. "When you're ready, I'll help you up so you can feed this little one and then if you want I'll take you upstairs to have a shower."

"That sounds like bliss." She smiles, and love overwhelms me.

It used to be that all I had was work, but now my life is so full that it's a lot to take in.

And it's all thanks to Cassie.

EPILOGUE

CASSIE

My life is so full.

Today's our first wedding anniversary.

Our girls are with Patrick's mother and for the first time since Charlotte was born, we get a whole night alone.

I'm so grateful for this life with Patrick's parents being a close part of our family.

Since we've been back together, Jane has stepped in as a surrogate mother to me. I didn't realise how much I've missed that figure in my life—I haven't had anyone in the position since Gran died.

But she loves our girls fiercely, as does Brian, and any opportunity they get to spend time with them, they grab with both hands.

Sophie loves having her grandparents around. They spoil her rotten, but she's still the same grounded girl that I raised for all those years. I'm so very proud of her.

We see lots of Lauren as well. She's had her struggles, but

she lives with Ethan now and she's happier than I've seen her in a very long time. Mark's death hit her very hard, but I'm confident that she will be stronger as a result.

Ethan adores her, and she might just finally end up with the family she always wanted.

"Happy anniversary, babe." Patrick kisses me softly. He hands me a large envelope.

I open it and pull a large brochure out. "An Auckland University Prospectus? What's this for?"

He smiles. "Applications open soon for the next medical intake. I think you should apply."

"I think I'm a little bit too old to go back to school."

Patrick shakes his head. "I want you to live your dream. I got the career I wanted, and now it's your turn."

I shake my head. "But Charlotte and Sophie …"

"Will be fine. You missed out on so much, and it's not fair."

"Patrick." Tears well in my eyes. "I never thought I'd get the chance."

He runs his thumb down my cheek. "Whatever you need, I'll do it. I want you to be able to spread your wings."

I place the Prospectus on the coffee table. "I'll think about it. Now, aren't you taking me out somewhere nice for dinner?"

He grins. "I had other ideas."

"I know what your ideas are like. I want to go out for dinner instead of cooking."

Patrick laughs. "We're going out. But I thought we might replicate our first date."

I frown. "Replicate our first date? We didn't really go anywhere. You kind of just invited me into your bed."

"Not that first date. Our *first* first date. Burger and a movie. I believe that Marvel have a new movie out."

I bark out a laugh. "Oh, *that* date. If I remember rightly, that was the night you first kissed me."

He leans closer. "I thought I could do more than just kiss you tonight."

"See I knew you had an ulterior motive."

"I always have an ulterior motive where you're concerned."

———

JUST LIKE WE did that first night, we sit and eat burgers and talk. It's funny, I got so used to life with Mark where we never really sat down and just talked. He lived life a mile a minute, and working physically, it wasn't uncommon for him to fall asleep in front of the television.

He was a good man, especially when it came to Sophie. So the weekends were usually full of things that we all did together.

Life with Patrick is a very different pace. We take turns cooking dinner, and when Patrick cooks, Sophie is usually not far behind. She loves being with her father, and he loves being with her. Our evenings are spent together, and while Sophie does her homework, Patrick and I will usually be on the couch side-by-side, watching television and talking about our day.

Sophie disappears to her grandparents some weekends. But this is the first weekend they've had both children, as Patrick didn't want to miss a thing when it came to Charlotte.

It's only the fact that it's our wedding anniversary tonight that made him let go a little.

We walk hand-in-hand into the movie theatre, finding seats at the back.

It doesn't take long before Patrick slides his arm around my shoulders and tugs me in tight. I turn my head and meet his gaze.

And just like all those years ago, he kisses me until I lose track of what's happening on screen. There is no one around us to say anything—just two people reliving the early days of the romance.

A romance that will never have an end.

Stand alones

For the Love of Chloe

Only Ever You

Taking Chances

The Friends Duet

Loving Rowan

Three Days

The Forever Series

Something Real

The Right One

Unexpected

Lifetime Series

In a Lifetime

In an Instant

In a Heartbeat

In the End

At the Start

ABOUT THE AUTHOR

Wendy Smith lives with her two children and three cats in Hastings, New Zealand, and she's not sure who's responsible for her grey hair. She's a multi-platform bestselling author, whose book In the End, written as Ariadne Wayne, was named one of Apple's best books of 2017. All her stories come with a quirky sense of humour, and she cries over everything.

Find me online
www.wendysmith.co.nz
wendy@wendysmith.co.nz